Praise for *The Ingredients of You and Me*

"With all the makings of a Hallmark movie, this story will delight small-town romance readers.", *Booklist*

"Satisfying... the true charm of this story is the path Parker takes to rediscovering her passion for baking with help from a cast of supporting characters that will make readers want to reach for the first two books in the series and look forward to future installments.", *Library Journal*

"Parker's journey through a transitional period is interesting, and her close relationships with her girlfriends add humor.", *Kirkus Reviews*

Praise for *Meet Me on Love Lane*

"A sweet exploration of what it means to come home again... With a relatable heroine, witty dialogue, and an idyllic setting, *Meet Me On Love Lane* is a contemporary romance that is essentially a Hallmark movie on paper. While it's perfect as a standalone, readers will enjoy visiting Hope Lake time and time again.", *Booklist*

"In the feel-good second installment of Bocci's Hopeless Romantics series... the idyllic setting is vividly rendered and Charlotte's personal growth as she builds a home for herself is handled with compassion. Readers will enjoy this sweet, fluffy tale that sits squarely at the intersection of romance and wom

"Filled with small-town charm and a sweet cast of characters.", *Woman's World (Best of Week Book Club pick)*

"A feel-good romance that will add a spring to your step and light a fire in your heart, *Meet Me on Love Lane* was a heartfelt follow up from one of my new favorite authors, Nina Bocci.", *Harlequin Junkie (4 1/2 stars)*

"With the sweetest cast of characters and a rich history to fall madly in love with, I dare you to resist the allure of Hope Lake. Especially with charmers like Cooper, Nick, and Henry strutting their stuff all over town. *Meet Me On Love Lane* is the perfect follow up to *On the Corner of Love and Hate*, with all the same sweetness and tear-jerking true love you can expect from Nina Bocci.", *Hypable*

FROM HOPE LAKE, WITH LOVE

FROM HOPE LAKE, WITH LOVE

NINA BOCCI

FROM HOPE LAKE, WITH LOVE
Published with assistance by Brower Literary & Management

ISBN: 978-1-7326143-5-2
ISBN: 978-1-7326143-6-9 (eBook)

For the family and friends that helped to create Hope Lake.

Prologue

My leg shook, a steady tap, tap, tap against Patricia's hardwood floor.

"Are you nervous?"

"No," I lied.

"Camille," she breathed a heavy sigh and set the proposal, *my* proposal, onto her desk. My boss, who is notorious for being a speed reader, was taking an unusually long time reading it. "You're a terrible liar. You've always been a terrible liar."

"Uh?" I raised an eyebrow.

"Just say thank you. It's one of your more admirable qualities," she quipped, tucking a piece of her thick grey hair behind her ear. Picking up the pages again, she smiled as her eyes began moving quickly.

But still no comments.

"The suspense is killing me," I said, shifting in the plush leather seat.

"Shhh." Another grin.

I shook my head. "You're doing this on purpose. You're making me squirm because this is my final hoorah with the magazine."

"As if," she said with a smirk.

Finally, after what seemed like an eternity, she set the papers down, folding her hands over them. "A few things."

I took a deep breath, hoping to steady my nerves.

"I'm so happy that you remembered about Hope Lake. That was years ago that we discussed it."

"Well, you said try something new. Traveling cross-country for a piece is about as new as I can get," I said honestly.

"You'll love it," she insisted. "Especially because it'll be decorated for Christmas when you arrive."

"I'm getting there the night after Thanksgiving," I responded, perplexed.

"And?"

"And, isn't that a bit early to be decorated for Christmas?"

Pushing out her chair, she came around her desk and leaned against the edge. "Cami, Hope Lake would decorate the day after Halloween if it could get away with it."

"You're talking about the town like it's a person."

She shrugged, looking thoughtfully at a framed photo that hung on her wall. I knew it was from a summer she spent at Hope Lake as a child. "It sort of is, I suppose. It's become a bit of a character. I think collectively the residents treat the town like it's a living, breathing thing they have to take care of."

"I suppose that's a good thing. Must be a huge reason for the reputation it has in the travel community."

Reaching behind her, she took the proposal and handed it to me. "I'm happy that you're doing this piece, but I would be doing the magazine an injustice if I didn't try and keep you here."

"I appreciate that but I need to try something new."

"I know, dear. Just know that the door is always open, Cami."

I stood, and pulled her into a hug. "I will forever be grateful for the start you gave me, Patricia."

When I pulled back, she was wiping a tear away. "Any last bits of advice?"

Slinging my bag over my shoulder, I walked to the door and waited for her piece of wisdom.

"Hope Lake has a way of enchanting people, Cami. Let yourself be swept away."

I

Chapter One

A California native's first experience with snow shouldn't have included driving a dodgy rental car through an unfamiliar state. Especially with the gas tank nearing empty. Yet, there I was, braving a wild snowstorm at the end of November.

Unless I totally misunderstood how seasons worked on the East Coast, something was seriously amiss. Snow was piled high against the sides of the highway, trees were barren and draped in the white stuff that was falling as fast as my windshield wipers were.

Patricia had said that the town embraced Christmas the second the turkey carcas was in the trash but I wasn't actually expecting to drive into the North Pole. "If I see a sled, or hear a ho, ho, ho, I'm turning around and heading back to the sun."

Christmas music was on a local radio station, a young voice happily singing about her list for Santa. Even with the blaring holiday tunes, I was struggling to stay awake at the wheel. The extra jingle wasn't cutting it.

I switched on the air conditioning and put all four windows down a few inches, which let in a rush of snow, but it helped. Shivering at the blast of cold, I turned off the radio as if somehow the silence would help me find my destination. Thankfully, snow had just slid off one of the green highway signs perched on the roadside indicating gas was available at the next exit. That was one thing off the list.

After fueling up and getting some snacks to last me until I got to town, I pulled back onto the highway just after a snowplow rumbled by.

Thank goodness!

Once my GPS recalculated, it alerted me that there were only another twenty miles on this stretch of highway. Driving behind the plow would add at least another half hour thanks to the slow and steady pace. After that, who knew how the roads would be once I got into town and off the state roads. Hope Lake was nestled in a deep valley, which meant the likelihood of things being plowed seemed... slim. My guess was booking a small sedan without snow tires or four-wheel drive was not my smartest move.

"I should have asked Santa for an upgrade," I groaned.

Exhaling, I sent out a couple good thoughts into the universe hoping that things wouldn't be doom and gloom when I arrived. I was used to buses, cabs, hell any kind of public transportation that made traveling easy. But none of that was in the cards where I was headed.

From what I researched, Hope Lake, a small town about two hours north of Philadelphia, was a must-see burgeoning tourist stop and perfect for the small-town feature that Patricia insisted we run monthly. I've never written small town pieces, always preferring the big city travel columns, plus, I didn't cover the East Coast. There was nothing wrong with it, of course, but the magazine had a long-time writer who covered hotels and B&Bs on the eastern seaboard. Small town was her cup of tea. I was West Coast, big cities and flashy hotels and, because there is a God, and She is good, Hawaii.

Maybe I took this assignment because I wanted to challenge myself with a piece that I never aimed for before, or maybe it was because I knew if it flopped, I was done at *American Adventures* anyway.

My hope, for Hope Lake, was to sit by the water, either the lake, or the river, I wasn't choosy, and write. Or maybe by a fire pit in the yard of the B&B I had booked. The only real pre-requisite was that I was inspired. The way Patricia talked about the town, I had high hopes for Hope Lake.

The inspiration had to be dynamite. For both the article, and for the book that I was hopefully going to finish, or start over for the third time, while I was away. I guess in my fantasy I didn't imagine it being freezing and snowing outside, but I knew I'd make it work.

"This town better be everything she promised," I mumbled and dug out another Twizzler from the bottom of the plastic bag.

By the time I made it into town, I was full of Twizzlers Strawberry Twists, a bag of onion rings, and two Dr. Peppers.

I was also lost.

Signs were mostly covered in snow, but I managed to work out where the town square would be by sheer dumb luck.

I may have been lost, but, I was also in the center of Whoville. Or, Christmas Vacation, or Bedford Falls. I half expected

George Bailey from *It's a Wonderful Life* to come careening around a corner, skidding on the falling snow and yelling about Clarence, his guardian angel.

Parking the car to what I thought was the side of the road, I turned off the ignition, bundled up as best I could and shuffled out into the snow filled town.

Oh.

My.

God.

I couldn't help but smile. It was as if my timing was for once perfect. Maybe it was like Patricia said, and the town was enchanting. It knew I was coming, and managed the perfect snowstorm to highlight the Christmas spirit.

It was as if I was in a shaken snowglobe. The snow swirled against my lame-excuse for winter footwear—a pair of high-top Converse that had seen better days. It didn't matter though as I stared at the lights, the bows, the massive sparkling ornaments, a smile dancing on my lips.

I've heard the phrase before, 'it looks like Christmas' but I wasn't sure I had ever *seen* what that exactly looked like. Most cities had a prettily-decorated tree with an angel on top or shaped lighting arrangements on telephone poles. It certainly helped usher in the holiday spirit but the sight didn't usually make me immediately want to sing carols, wrap presents and bake cookies.

Hope Lake *looked* like Christmas. It *felt* like Christmas and I was only there for ten minutes.

It wasn't a cheap or tacky holiday display but like a thousand of Santa's most highly-skilled elves traveled from the

North Pole to decorate every inch of the town's square perfectly.

I found myself in the center of the most magical wonderland. Ornately decorated wreaths hung from each of the old-fashioned lamp posts. Warm, yellowy-white lights twinkled softly in the falling snow. A foot-wide holiday red bow was hanging in the center of two of the lampposts, long tails swaying in the breeze.

There was a fountain in the center of the square with six tall white pillars surrounding it. Each pole swirled with red ribbon to look like a candy cane. From the each top, thick green ivy was wrapped in the same white lights and the garland swagged between the poles.

In the center of the square stood a beautiful, full and well-decorated fir tree. Nothing the size of Rockefeller Center of course, but it was still proud and perfectly placed so that it could seen from anywhere around the square.

"I wonder when they'll light the star?" I whispered, my breath showing in puffs of cold air before me. Considering it was only the day after Thanksgiving, I figured not for a bit. Hopefully, I would be able to see it while I was here.

"Tomorrow night," a strong female voice said from beside me.

I jumped, stumbling back toward a drift of snow that had blown against the fountain.

"Sorry, dear. I thought you heard me shuffling along in the snow," the woman explained. "You'll catch your death out here dressed like that. Come on over to the bakery, we'll get you fixed up with something warm to drink and a plate of treats."

My initial reaction was to say 'no, thanks' but I was lost

and still hungry even after a bag full of unhealthy food. "That's kind, thanks," I said, following the woman back through the tracks she had made.

She was quite tall, and dressed in a chic winter coat with a gorgeous faux fur collar pulled up to her ears. "Where are we going?" I asked, thinking I should have questioned her before agreeing to follow a stranger. But what could a little old lady do to me?

When we reached a brightly lit shop, a bakery if I had to guess judging by the large muffin, loaf of bread and cupcake etched into the glass door, a few women were piling into a large black SUV that was idling at the curb. I couldn't see the driver from my vantage point, but they beeped when they saw us coming.

A diminutive elderly woman with sleek gray hair and a wry smile was leaving out of the front door as we approached and ushered me inside, tsking when she saw what I was wearing. Needless to say, I wasn't prepared for snow.

"Come, dear, you'll catch a cold," the woman who had met me outside said, and pointed to a chair near the window.

Settling in, I pulled my coat tighter around me but snow plopped onto the floor near my soaking sneakers. I didn't realize how wet I had gotten in the snowfall.

A woman in a motorized wheelchair zipped up beside me and quickly began barking orders. "Viola, get a cocoa and some cookies and maybe another blanket, and, Mancini, try and look like you're being productive."

The old leather chair that I sank into was the perfect combination of worn in and supportive and I realized just how exhausted I was from a full day of traveling. All I wanted was a toasty fire in the hearth, my favorite blanket and a glass of wine. Instead, I had a room full of adorable strangers.

"What is this place?" I asked, unable to read the name on the sign that was hanging above front window on the other side of the shop.

"This, is The Baked Nanas," the woman in the motorized chair said, handing me a thick, long cardigan sweater. "Here, your coat is soaked, this will help take the chill out of your bones."

"Thanks." I slipped the wet coat off. The woman that had met me out in the snow took it, and hung it on a coat rack near an old-fashioned radiator in the corner. "I appreciate it."

On her way back toward us, she grabbed a plate of cookies, and offered it to me along with. I thanked her, and warmed my hands on the sides.

The three women were huddled together at an antique-looking wrought iron bistro table with lovely, colorful padded seats that had snowmen on them.

Like the town square, this shop was classically decorated for the holidays. A small tree was in the corner, this time with large, old-fashioned colored bulbs in green, blue and red. Atop it sat a delicate angel with wide, white wings.

Garland was artistically draped around the front door, and the two street-facing windows were covered in soft colorful lights.

"You guys sure like Christmas here, huh?"

"You could say that," a woman with inky black hair that defied gravity and the brightest yellow tracksuit said.

I set the mug down on the dainty table beside me and looked up at the women—my curious, and nearly silent, audience—the only sound was coming from the low Christmas music playing in the background.

"While I don't necessarily mind being stared at, it appears you have some questions? I mean, this *is* an odd situation, I'm sure. Or perhaps, if I have overstayed my welcome, I could see myself out," I asked and began folding the blanket up that was on my lap.

"You're more than welcome to stay. Our meeting is over but we aren't leaving just yet, we're waiting for our rides, and yes we have so many questions," the woman from outside said animatedly with her hand in the air. She was possibly the youngest of the group with long dark hair and a blouse that left little to the imagination.

I glanced at my watch. It was nearly eight and the roads were getting awful. Granted, I had no idea how to drive in the snow, but considering their median age was seventy, I didn't think it was safe for them on the roads, either.
"Okay, what type of questions?" I asked, wondering what the meeting that I interrupted was about.

They began whispering among themselves.

"Sorry we're being rude, it's not every day that a California girl drops in on Hope Lake. Especially out of the blue. We're used to the New Yorkers or the Philly crowd. Glowing and tan at the end of November isn't a common appearance in this neck of the woods," the one woman said, her voice raspy and strong which was at odds with her fragile appearance in her bright red wheelchair. "I'm Dr. Imogen Bishop, but call me Gigi, everyone in town does."

I leaned forward in the chair, angling the folded blanket awkwardly over my tanned, bare legs. Not my smartest move when I boarded the plane, but I was expecting mild fall not frozen tundra. "Gigi," I began, smiling at her Rolling Stones t-shirt she had underneath a thick cardigan sweater. "Nice to meet you. How'd you figure California?"

With a glint in her eye, she, too, leaned forward, albeit slowly, given her difficulty in her wheelchair. "Sun-kissed hair with beachy waves, sparkling eyes, and a late-fading tan. And you're wearing shorts in November. Screams California girl. Am I wrong?"

I shook my head. "Correct. Born and raised in San Francisco. I'm impressed."

She preened. "It's a gift."

"More like a party trick," Yellow Tracksuit said. "Give her a minute, she'll have you pegged for dating status, employment, and who knows what else."

"Impressive trick, Gigi. What else can you tell me?" Leaning back, I covered up with the blanket again and folded my hands over my crossed legs.

Her sharp gray eyes started at my wayward hair, easing over my face, where she paused just a moment before carrying on. She spent an inordinate amount of time on my hands, which made them sweat a bit under her scrutiny. There was no way that this woman, Gigi, who had to be in her eighties, would squirrel out anything about me outside of what my sunny appearance gave away.

She took a deep breath, and the others leaned in. Tracksuit had a devilish smirk and placed a five-dollar bill on the small table in front of them that was strewn with used mismatched coffee cups and plates filled with crumbs and forks. The other three followed suit, each tossing five bucks onto the table.

"Should I put in a fiver, too?" I asked, reaching for my pocket.

Tracksuit smiled. "Sure if you'd like. It's just a bit of a side hustle that we do when Gigi does her little trick. The money goes into the pot for beer and pizza night over at Casey's."

Nodding, and a bit taken aback that they have a pizza and beer night at their age, I threw the money on the counter and sat back. "Ready when you are, Gigi."

She looked wildly confident with her round, bright green glasses and sharp eyes twinkling behind them. She smiled before rubbing her chin. "You said San Francisco, but I don't quite think you were raised there. Somewhere on the outskirts, perhaps. Berkley? No, Stanford for college, I think. English major but possibly anthropology. I don't think journalism, but it could be. I can't narrow it down. You're a researcher or a writer, or want to be a writer. Recently single, and while not ready to mingle, you're not opposed to it. Only child, parents are supportive but disappointed you're not a lawyer."

I snorted. "Judge, actually. Both of my folks are lawyers in Palo Alto. They had their hopes on a SCOTUS seat someday. Stanford, both English *and* anthropology. Travel writer, and you're a damn marvel."

The woman in the tracksuit guffawed. "Never fails. I swear we can take this act on the road," she said.

Gigi laughed. "It's a gift, and, no, Suzanne, you're a shitty driver. We can't take anything on the road."

"Well, I'm impressed," the one who had met me in the snow said. She appeared to be the youngest of the three and just as hilariously outfitted as the other two. "I'm Sophia, and I recently lost my license, so I'm not driving, either."

"That's a story I'd like to hear," I said honestly.

"Short version is that I'm also a terrible driver."

Sophia stood, walked over, and shook my hand. "Since our little show-and-tell is over, maybe we can have a normal conversation and you can give us a little something yourself? Like, your name?"

I turned to Gigi. "Any guesses?"

She laughed, zipping the chair over to my side of the shop. "No, pulling names out of thin air is a little too Las Vegas for my parlor tricks. I'm just observant. Nice to meet you."

I shook her hand gently. "That was more than observant, it was crystal-ball level magic," I said, standing and letting the blanket fall to the chair. "I'm Camille. It's nice to meet you, too."

"So, Camille, what brings you to Hope Lake?" Tracksuit asked. She was cleaning up the table, bringing cups to the area behind the counter.

"I think it's interesting how people show up in Hope Lake these days," Sophia said.

"Really? Why's that?" I asked, pulling out my phone and opening the notes app. It was never too early to get a base for the article. The senior circuit was always known for spreading choice gossip, and I had a feeling that this particular band of girlfriends spilled the best tea.

"Oh, well let's see," Sophia began, adjusting the pillow at her back. Before she spoke, she looked side to side as if she were about to whisper state secrets.

"Charlotte, the florist, she owns that shop right over there," she said, pointing behind me.

I turned to see where she was pointing to. Across the way was another shop that boasted floor-to-ceiling glass windows identical to the ones here. Whereas this one had *The Baked Nanas* etched into the glass now that I knew what I was reading, those windows said *Late Bloomers* in a decorative font. You couldn't see much of the shop itself because it was only lit by low security lighting.

"Charlotte, huh? What's her story?" I asked eagerly. Upon hearing the conversation, Tracksuit made her way back over to her respective chair to listen in.

Let the tea spilling commence.

"I'll take this one, Sophia," Gigi said, zipping her chair back over to my side. She looked longingly at the shop behind me, her eyes brimming with tears. "The Charlotte in question is Charlotte Bishop," she said with a small smile at her lips. "My granddaughter."

"I see. So, her story is interesting enough to share?" I asked, trying not to sound too eager. Sure, I was a travel writer, but getting quirky anecdotes for a story was just as good as anything. They gave heart and humanity to the article so it wouldn't just be the dos and don'ts of the town, what to see, where to eat. Otherwise, if I didn't use it for the article, I would squirrel the information away for the book—a women's fiction romance about a woman traveling to find herself. I supposed it could have been an auto-biograpahy.

"I don't want to pry, of course."

Gigi nodded sagely. "You're not prying. If you spend twenty seconds or more in town, you'll hear about her. Charlotte left as a young girl, and only returned a couple years ago. Needless to say, it was quite the entrance back. That's what they meant by an interesting return. There have been many people—Charlotte, Reese, Parker—have came for odd reasons and yet have all ended up staying."

The other two nodded in agreement.

"It all worked out in the end. She's engaged to her sweetie. They have quite the love story. He owns the bookstore across the square there, and he's a teacher up at the high school," Tracksuit pointed into the swirling storm. "You'll meet him when he comes to pick us up in a bit."

"That reminds me, is Charlotte going to be doing the flowers for the event next week?"

And I lost them. They continued making plans and chatting as if I was already part of their group. Which again felt like a testament to small-town life. They included you, even as a stranger.

I held up my hand like I was a schoolgirl trying to get the teacher's attention. It felt rude, but they were all rambling, and I couldn't get a word in edgewise.

"I'm sorry, if I can interrupt for a moment. I feel impossibly rude, but aside from Sophia, and Gigi, I don't know your name. In my head, I'm calling you Tracksuit," I said, pointing to the unknown woman with the jet-black hair and bright pink lipstick.

The woman that I was mentally referring to as Tracksuit guffawed so loudly that I was convinced someone could have heard the sound over the blustering winds outside. "New nickname, girls—Tracksuit!"

Grateful that she wasn't mad, I laughed at the fact that

they referred to themselves as *girls*. Though, I suppose they were in their own minds. My friends at home had girls' nights once a month, and we were all over forty.

"I saw your other compatriots leaving earlier. You mentioned a meeting?"

Sophia, piped up. "We all have a hand, or two in something around Hope Lake, including The Baked Nanas. I'm also mom to my amazing daughter, Emma, and Nonnie to an amazing little boy named Sebastian. My son-in-law, Cooper, is the mayor, and my husband is the former mayor."

"Yeah, yeah, it's not all about you, Sophia," Tracksuit teased and carried on as if she hadn't been interrupted. "Gigi, she was the town doc for what, a hundred years or so, and now her son is the current doctor," she said, and then she puffed up her chest and smiled. "And I'm Suzanne Mancini, but you only get to call me Mancini or Tracksuit from now on, and while I don't have a job, per se, I'm in everyone's business," she said, with a smile.

"That sounds like a full-time job to me, Mancini," I said, hoping to keep the conversation coming from them and not have it aimed at me, but that wish was not granted.

"So," Gigi said, driving her wheelchair back over to the ladies. They sat a bit like a three-person jury, all lined up facing me as if I were their witness.

"Is this where you gang up on me and lull me into submission, so I expose all my little flaws and secrets?"

Gigi looked affronted, resting her hand against her throat. "Now, dear. Do we look like we would do that?"

I gave them all a solid once-over. They weren't short on the adorable looks that you got from the elderly. Sweet smiles, and glassy tear-filled eyes but these ladies were pros and I loved it. Underneath it all, they seemed to love their gossip.

Who didn't?

"As a matter of fact, yes."

"You're right, we'll pester and poke until you give in. Sometimes, it's just easier to confess everything all at once," Sophia encouraged.

"Well, that's a bit of a story. Funnily enough, I came here *for* a story, and to finish a book, and that's about all the dirty details I have." I took a sip of my now-cool cocoa.

"How did you end up here? Not in Hope Lake, but *here*."

I smiled. "My phone died, and with it, so did the directions to the B&B I booked a room at. Since sleeping in my car in the middle of a snowstorm wasn't high on my list of things to check off, I followed the lights thinking something here would be open and I could ask for help."

"We want to hear how you chose Hope Lake of all places, but we also need to get you to the B&B and adjusted to east coast time. Where is your car?" Maninci asked.

I stood and walked toward the front door. "Over there, um, somewhere?" I pointed generically toward the square where I left the rental. Even from the distance, I could see that it was covered in snow. "It's not exactly a stellar snow vehicle. I probably should have just kept driving until I found it, but I've never driven in the snow."

Gigi pulled out her iPhone and tapped away quickly. "We'll get you there, don't worry. You can leave the car there, and someone will get it for you tomorrow after the roads get plowed. For now, we'll drive you."

"Don't fret, you'll be fine, if you're worried about traveling.

It's not very far, and we've got big trucks, snow tires and chains," Mancini explained. "We'll grab whatever luggage you've got and take that over, too. In case you can't get out tomorrow, either. We're expected to get quite a bit of snow the next couple days. So, better not leave anything in the car."

"You're going to drive? In this?" My eyes widened, thinking of how they'd just told me they were awful drivers.

"Heavens, no." Mancini tapped away on her own phone. "We have that covered. Our boyfriends come to pick us up."

"This I have to see," I mumbled and began rearranging the chairs in an effort to make myself useful. I had no idea where anything went, so I followed Sophia's lead.

"They're outside," Gigi said, zipping over to the coat rack in the corner and pulling off the thick wool coat on the very bottom hook.

"You can ride with Reese. He'll make sure to grab your things from the rental car and get you all situated over at the B&B." Mancini ushered us toward the door, throwing my still-damp coat toward me. "Keep the sweater, you're going to need it!"

Once I got outside, I realized it was still snowing. While I was pulling on the coat, I miscalculated my next step and the amount of snow. Before I knew it, I ended up falling right into the arms of a tall, Black man that gave strong Idris Elba vibes, who caught me easily before I could slide across the snowy sidewalk.

2

Chapter Two

"Woah there. Watch the ice," he quipped. It wasn't the smoothest of lines, but, I laughed regardless. He made sure I was steady before removing his hands. "Good?" he asked, smoothing his gloved hand across his chin.

"I am, thanks," I said. "Thanks for the save."

His mouth turned up in a half-smile. "My pleasure. I'll be back for you in a second. I have to secure the precious cargo." He gently moved me to the side and joined two other men that were near the sidewalk. Gigi, in her motorized chair, waited patiently for the handsome man with a beard to open the door to a Jeep that boasted four massive tires.

"Is that her granddaughter's boyfriend?" I asked Mancini who was standing beside me, holding onto my arm for support.

"Yes, that's Henry. He and Charlotte live with Gigi in the big house. Usually she likes to go with Nick, he's the one over there in the pickup truck and the ridiculous light bar on the front."

I looked to where she pointed. A large, silver pick up truck with monster tires and chains wrapped around them was next to the curb. The front bumper was lined with bright spot lights as if it was about to drive into the jungle at night.

"That's absurd but also it seems sort of fun in a silly way."

Mancini nodded. "That's why Gigi likes to go with him. His horn is loud and goofy, the light inside used to be a disco light but Chief Birdy told him it was a distraction so he had to take it out."

"So they're here to take you guys home?"

"Yes. We're so grateful. We'd be miserable if we had to stay home everytime it snows. Now listen," she said, turning to me. The other two were securely in the vehicles, Gigi with Henry and Sophia with Nick. That left Mancini and I.

"Are we going with him?" I asked, pointing to the man striding toward us. The same who had saved me from falling on my rear earlier.

Mancini winked. "No, Gigi and I live next door to each other so I'll hitch a ride with little Henry," she said, pointing to the man who was well over six feet.

"He's little?"

She ignored me and held up a finger to the gentleman. He stopped a few feet a way giving us a bit of privacy.

"Reese will get you to the B&B safe and sound and we'll check in tomorrow to see what you're up to and get the rest of your story. How long are you staying for?" she asked and waved the man over. I assumed the man was Reese.

"About a month, give or take. I don't really have definite plans," I said. The book could take a month, or five to complete.

"Oh, open-ended plans. Those are our favorite kinds," she exclaimed and clapped her hands gleefully. "Remember I'm Mancini to you, or Tracksuit!"

She laughed the entire way to the car, and when the man she referred to as Nick helped her up into Henry's truck, she gave him a big, loud kiss on his cheek.

The temperature had dipped to a biting degree, making it worse when the wind picked up.

"Well, they are certainly prepared," I said absently, pulling my borrowed sweater tighter around my chest.

Reese tapped his heavy boots together like Dorothy trying to return home. "Yes, the ladies are persistent to put it mildly. They want what they want and frankly, I'm not big enough of a man to tell them no."

He looked plenty big from where I was standing—broad shoulders and a fit body, even beneath the heavy sweater and thick coat. I was on the taller side, and he had at least six inches or more on me.

"Ready?" he asked with a smile.

"I guess it's just us?"

He nodded, a small smile lifting his lips. Handsome. It was a simple word to describe a man, but sometimes, it was all you needed. Thick dark eyebrows framed his expressive deep brown eyes, that glinted in the streetlights. He wasn't freshly shaven, instead his dark skin sported a bit of a grey and black shadow on his angular jaw.

"No gloves?" he asked, and immediately pulled his off and stuffed them onto my hands. "Come on, the B&B isn't that far but we have to go toward the lake and none of those roads have been plowed yet.

"How do you know?" I asked. "Do you live over that way?"

He laughed, deep and raspy. "You can say that. I'm Maxwell, but I prefer Max. Reese is just what my girls call me."

My girls.

I held out my now-gloved hand. "Nice to meet you, Maxwell Reese. I'm Camille. But you can call me Cami."

As we started walking, I tried not giving him a once-over, but we were the only two people on an otherwise deserted sidewalk and his profile was definitely nice to admire.

He helped me into the SUV, closing the door behind me. As he walked around the front, he wiped the snow off of the headlights. When he joined me, settling into the driver's seat, he turned and smiled.

"So, Cami," he said, pushing the ignition button. "What brings you to Hope Lake?"

"Wow," I breathed, settling into the seat. "You guys don't waste any time getting to the nitty gritty do you."

His eyes grew wide. "I apologize, I didn't—"

"I'm kidding. It's fine. I'm a perfect stranger in your town. I'd ask questions too," I insisted.

Pulling away from the curb, he drove slowly over the snow-covered road. "Where's the car?"

I squinted. "Over there? I think? The white Ford something or other. It's the least snow-friendly car I think I could have rented."

He chuckled and again I was struck by how deep his voice was. "You wait here. I'll grab your things."

"Oh, no, I can help."

Max glanced down at my bare legs and raised an eyebrow. "I insist."

Pulling on a knit hat, he grabbed another pair of gloves from the center console and slid out into the snow. When the door opened, the wind kicked up again ushering another blast of cold and snow into the car until he slammed it shut.

"Jesus," I said, unlocking the car for him and pulling my coat down as much as I could to cover my legs.

Max made quick work of my suitcases and laptop bag, carrying everything back to the car in one trip. Piling it into the backseat, he looked up at me on the passenger side. He disappeared again, this time to the back of the truck, opening the rear access. Grabbing something, he walked back around to my side and opened the door.

"This might help until we can get you to the B&B and by the fires," he said, offering me a thick flannel blanket.

I grabbed onto it as if it were the last cookie in the jar and wrapped it around my legs. "Thank you," I said as soon as he was in the truck.

"You're welcome. Admittedly, the outfit makes me even more curious as to why you're here, dressed like that, in this." He said the last bit with a grand flourish toward the blustery snow.

I took stock of what I was wearing. Shorts that hit mid-thigh and a light, flowy Bohemian-style blouse. The cardigan that the ladies had given me at the bakery was the only other sensible thing that was fitting for the weather besides the jacket I bought at the airport when I landed. I realize now, for a travel writer, how idiotic I was when packing. I knew better to research where I was going but I was so eager to get here

I just through clothes into my suitcase without thought and got on a plane.

"So? You're visiting?" he asked, as he pulled out onto the deserted street.

Due to the lack of plowing, or maybe just because the snow was falling faster than they could get it off the roads, he had to stay in the center of the street where it was at least slightly safer.

"I'm here for work, you could say. My editor," I began, not bothering to add *former* to the explanation, "went to college around here and suggested running a piece on the town. I freelance for a travel magazine. Aside from that, I've got a novel that I'd like to finish so I figured two birds, and all that jazz."

He carefully wound through the streets, sitting quietly as I rambled. It's not that I was nervous, just a smidge uneasy thanks to the weather.

"I never would have found my way to the B&B. The amount of snow that has fallen is unbelievable. I don't recognize a thing from earlier."

"Is this the way you came in?"

I nodded. "I know it is, but wow, it's crazy how fast it changed."

"The weather is always a tricky thing in the valley." His tone was bland, yet he didn't appear to be someone that would be boring. At least not under normal circumstances.

"Music?" he asked, pushing the button before I responded.

"Sure," I said quietly, smiling when I realized the same song from earlier was on again.

As we drove, I mentally added up the amount of decorations strewn about town. Everything seemed to be expertly decorated and yet, it never seemed like it was *too* much.

"I'm out of sorts, I think. It was just Thanksgiving, literally, and this place is a wonderland. Don't you get sick of it by the time it's Christmas?"

He shook his head. "I don't. I'm sure some do, but nothing beats Hope Lake at Christmas."

"We'll see if I agree in a month's time."

He only smiled in response. '

"You know, the bakery detour was an accident. My intention was to head straight to the B&B, have something to eat, and get unpacked. Go to bed early and get my body on East Coast time."

"Do you travel a lot?" he asked.

I studied his profile, then glanced at his gloved hands but I couldn't see if there was a ring.

"So, do you?" he asked again, and I shifted in the seat.

"Sorry, I zoned out. I do, yes. Mostly West Coast, sometimes Australia and Asia. There's another writer who lives in New York who keeps track of this side of the country. She's been with the magazine since its inception. Someone else is in Europe. We're all spread out to make it easier."

"Sounds like a busy life. You're able to stay here for a little bit? Your booking said a month."

I glanced at him. "How'd you know that?"

He tapped the wheel for a second. "Small town, you know." He winked and turned onto a long gravel path. On the side of the road was a large sign that read Hope Lake Bed-and-Breakfast

Below that was the proprietor's name, but it was covered

in snow. "I hope you don't live far since you did me a favor by bringing me all this way out here. I didn't realize how bad the roads were."

He smiled. "I'm nearby."

The scene before me was something I imagined was on a postcard for this place back in the day. The bed-and-breakfast must have been a grand family estate at some point then divided up when someone transformed it into this. It was a massive two-story brick home with four tall, stately ivory columns at the entrance. Like the ones in town, these were decorated as candy canes, with thick, red ribbon wrapped around them. An enormous wreath was placed between the second story windows, lit up with what seemed to be thousands of twinkly white lights.

To the side of the main home was a two-car wide carport or turn around that I assumed was for guests. On either side were two well-lit Christmas trees in planters. The white lights welcomed us to the B&B. Max pulled his car under the carport, threw it into park, and turned off the engine.

"We're here."

I looked around the otherwise empty parking lot. "I guess I didn't pick tourist season, huh?"

He shook his head. "You're about four months too early. There's a staff, of course. But it's minimal this time of year. I can promise that you'll be well taken care of while you're here."

I side-eyed him. "How could you know that?"

He opened the car door, slid out and stood facing me with a smile. "Because I own it."

3

Chapter Three

"Didn't anyone think to mention that?" I asked, trying not to laugh at what was such an obvious omission.

He carried my luggage into the reception area with me hot on his heels. Soft Christmas music played over the speakers, and the entire area smelled like warm cinnamon sugar. He set everything down by a large, ornate oak desk that held a single lamp, a phone, and a thick leather book with a gold ribbon sticking out of it. Behind the desk was a small Christmas tree and tiny presents beneath it.

"Marjorie?" he called, and we were joined by a petite Black woman with long, salt-and-pepper hair that was pulled back into a low side ponytail. She was starting to hunch over slightly, much like some of the ladies from earlier did. She wore a bright pink scarf wrapped around her head like a bandana and had clear framed cheetah glasses with small pink jewels at the corners.

She smiled brightly upon seeing me standing beside Max. He received a curious look and raised an eyebrow, similar to what he had done earlier. I looked between them but dismissed the feeling.

"Hello, dear. You must be Camille Douglas. I'm happy to meet you. Maxwell will take your things upstairs for you once I get you your key."

"Oh no, that's okay," I insisted, pulling my bag from his shoulder. "I don't have much. I'm sure you're busy with. . .things."

He huffed. "Marjorie, please tell Cami that I'm never too busy to make a guest feel welcome."

"Cami?" she parroted, and gave him another grin. "I insist that he helps. He has to earn his keep around here somehow."

I flattened my lips. "Of course, I just don't want anyone to put themselves out. Max already drove me all the way here. I'm sure he's got to get home?"

Marjorie raised her eyebrow. "Maxwell, maybe you can check on Ross. See if he can warm up dinner for you both," she offered.

My stomach answered for me. "Thanks, Marjorie."

"Oh, and I hope you like your décor. Usually, we don't decorate the guest rooms but I thought it would be a nice touch since you're the only one here."
I smiled. "That was kind, thanks. I'm sure I'll love it."

Max excused himself, and left my things on a bench next to the check in desk, stacking them neatly into a sturdy pile. "He's very precise, I'm guessing," I said to myself.

"He is, but I suppose that goes with the jobs."

"Jobs? Plural?"

"Did he tell you anything?" she said, not exactly sounding surprised.

Now that I thought of it, no. "He asked very specific questions, or but he wasn't very verbose, no." I didn't get the impression that he wasn't interested in what I was saying. He listened and responded.

"Perhaps he's not someone that opens up to strangers," I mused. I could understand that but in my line of work, I had to pull facts and information out of people. Max wouldn't be any different.

Marjorie didn't miss a beat in filling me in. "He's one of the doctors in town. He joined Dr. Bishop's practice. So, accuracy, efficiency, timeliness. They're all positive attributes to have in both lines of work. Especially with how much he has going on."

"What else does he have going on?" I said, intrigued by the good doctor's apparently busy schedule.

She tapped the pen. "The practice takes up a bit of time, and he's always helping out in neighboring towns. He and Dr. Bishop are the first to jump in when needed."

I leaned on the counter. "This place is busy? I looked it up before booking, you've got great reviews in the last year or so, so you're doing something right."

She beamed. "That's Maxwell for you," she said absently as she scribbled in the book.

"No computer? Or anything to keep track besides a book?" That wasn't very modern, though the reset of the amenities didn't seem lacking at all.

Marjorie scrunched up her nose. "Yes, there is. It's in the back for the other staff to use. I am not a fan and since it's the slow season, I do my own thing. I like this book. It suits me just fine."

"I like a woman that knows what she wants," I teased.

Even though her head was still down as she wrote notes in the log book, I could see her smile. "When Maxwell first bought this place, and wanted me to come to help out, I insisted on keeping some of the charm. It worked fine for thirty years, why change a good thing."

I shrugged. "You've got a point."

"It wasn't in the best condition before he bought it. People were very hard on the old owners – I think that's why it was such a steal."

Where Max was the silent type, Marjorie seemed willing to share anything.

"Marjorie, you know I'm a writer, right? I won't add anything that you divulge unless you're okay with it."

She shrugged. "It's not like anything I'm saying is a secret. Ask anyone in Hope Lake and they'll tell you the same thing."

I made a mental note of the character of the building, the antiquated, yet charming, way of checking people in and how sweet and helpful Marjorie was. While I thought I could sit and chat with her about the B&B, Hope Lake and even, perhaps, Max, it was late, and she looked exhausted.
"I'm pre-paid, right? If you'd like to turn in, I can find my own way to the room?" I offered, but she brushed me off as she fought off a yawn.

"You're sweet. I usually never turn in until I know Maxwell is home safe, but today has gotten the best of me."

"It's no problem. I'd feel better if I knew you were resting. I really don't mind."

"I don't know what's keeping him. I'm surprised he's not out trying to help plow or shovel roads. It must still be coming down," she said, looking out the large front windows at the still falling snow.

"Wait, does Max live here, too?" I asked, looking around the lobby area. Sure enough, there was a door off to the side that said private. It could easily lead to a second floor, or something else.

"Yes, of course. He really didn't tell you a thing." Marjorie said as she handed a key over to me. An actual key. Not a key card that needed programming. An honest-to-God brass key, with a little tag on it that said the number ten.

"There's another wing just through that door. I have the whole first floor. It's a bit much for me, but Maxwell insisted that I be comfortable."

"That's convenient," I said, smiling when she patted my hand. "Just point me in the right direction, and I'll be fine."

She smiled gratefully. "I put you on the second floor, right by the window at the end of the hallway. You'll be able to see the sunrise over the lake and there is a cozy sitting area with a window seat. Since we're empty, you'll have that whole corner to yourself," she said kindly, handing me a small packet with my receipt on top of the stack.

My handwritten receipt.

"You're just darling, has anyone ever said that?" I said, patting her hand gently.

"Aren't you sweet. My husband used to tell me I was a darling. It's funny that you used that exact word. Now, you head up. I'll have Max bring your things, and Ross will be up with a chicken pot pie for you."

"I didn't think you guys served dinner?"

She smiled. "We don't. We had something delivered for

you for when you arrived. Ross is in charge of the menu for the guests but you're the only guest, and since you can't go out or get delivery—" She broke off for another yawn, "we thought we would have something here for you since it's so late."

How thoughtful. "Good night, Marjorie. Thank you for the hospitality. I really appreciate it."

She gave a small wave before disappearing into through the door marked private.

Left to my own devices, and not ready to turn in just yet, I wandered the main floor just a bit. In the center of the room was a grand staircase. Loops, and dips of the same thick, ever-green garland and tiny twinkling lights danced up the railing leading to the top where a massive tree stood proudly.

The woodwork was off-white like the columns out front, the runner up the middle was a bright, cheery yellow. Though I didn't think I was tired, my bones felt weary as I climbed to the second story, but when I turned around to look over the railing, I was greeted with a beautiful sight of the lower level. A fieldstone fireplace graced one wall, with a large railroad tie for a mantlepiece. It too had garland hung with care as well as three wide brass candle holders with ivory tapers just waiting to be lit.

In front of the hearth was a navy loveseat and two Queen Anne chairs surrounding an oak coffee table stacked with what looked like vintage Christmas books. There were small two- or four-person tables near the windows with more books stacked in the center of each as decoration.

It was all homey and comfortable, all while embracing the perfect holiday look. Some B&B's tended to be stuffy, or old-fashioned but this felt classic. I couldn't wait to snap photos of my own as the ones that I found online did not do it justice. That was something I would speak to Max about before I wrote my article on my stay.

Wandering down the hall, I made mental notes, wishing that I had taken my bag with the notebook in it to jot ideas down. By the time I ended up at number ten, I wasn't sure if I even had the energy for dinner—until I smelled it.

Turning, I spied a tall, lanky older man with thinning dark brown hair carrying a wide rectangular tray with the tell-tale silver dome in the center. "You must be Ross," I said as a greeting.

He smiled. "I am, and you must be Ms. Douglas. It's a pleasure."

I hurried to retrieve the key and get the door open. Fumbling around for the switch, I turned on the lights, and gasped. "Oh!" I blurted, seeing the room all lit up.

"These rooms are something," he said, setting the tray down on the table near the coffee pot. "When Max bought the B&B, he and Marjorie went through the whole place and made some pretty spectacular changes."

"I'll say."

Ross moved toward the door and gave a small wave.

"Night. Thank you."

I took the lid from the tray and breathed in deeply. The pot pie smelled divine, and it was still warm as if straight from the oven. It was thankfully in a deep bowl that allowed me to carry it around the room while I ate and admired my new digs for the next however long.

The room was larger than I anticipated and I realized

quickly that it wasn't what I booked, instead upgraded to a suite. Something that I would need to thank them for tomorrow. It was an open concept with a small living area that overlooked what I assumed was the lake Marjorie mentioned. To the side near the door was a small refrigerator, a hot plate, and a small sink. I wouldn't call it an efficiency, per se, but it was definitely going to be handy. Around the corner was a bathroom with a claw foot tub, and a beautiful white, marble vanity.

But the crowning glory was the bedroom. Thankfully the wide, white door was closed so I got the full effect when I opened it. There was a small side lamp near the four-poster bed. Queen sized and covered in pillows. There was a window seat, and a Queen Anne chair similar to the one in the hallway. A navy blanket was draped over it, and there was a small table beside it with a book and an unlit candle.

Just as Marjorie promised, it was simply decorated for the holidays with tiny accents throughout the room.

If I weren't so tired and hungry, I would sit in the chair by the window with the santa pillow and wait for the sun to come up.

A soft rap at the door halted my plan to crawl into bed with my pot pie and sleep until morning.

"Coming," I called, padding into the main room and setting down the pot pie.

I opened the door to find a tired-looking Max waiting with all of my things. "I'm sorry you had to carry all of this. I would have come back down."

"May I?" he asked, expectantly looking behind me.

"Oh, yes, sorry," I rambled and stepped aside.

Much like he had downstairs on the bench, he arranged all of my bags neatly on the floor near the couch.

"Everything okay?"

I nodded. "More than. You didn't need to give me a suite."

"Why not? You're the only one here," he said plainly.

"Good point. Either way, I'm grateful."

"Need anything else?"

"No, I'm good," I answered, realizing that even though I was tired, and he too was clearly exhausted, I wanted to continue talking to him. Though, it seemed, I'd be doing most of the talking.

"Thanks, Max. You've been very helpful."

He smiled. "I appreciate that. Make sure you tell Marjorie; I can use the brownie points."

"Oh, yeah? For what?" I said eagerly, jumping on the smidge of openness.

"Actual brownies," he quipped. "She makes the best peanut butter chocolate brownies that you'll ever eat. Promise."

My eyes widened. "They sound sinful. I'll give you a glowing review tomorrow. The packet she gave me mentioned light breakfast and tea in the sunroom at nine. Will you be around for that?" I said, knowing that I could get some information out of him. "I know the ladies mentioned dropping by if the weather lets up."

"They probably won't make it tomorrow. Perhaps the next day, though. They never miss Thursday tea with Marjorie. The snow is supposed to come down all night and tomorrow."

"So, morning tea?" I asked again, hoping that I didn't sound eager.

He grinned. "Afraid not. I have to be in town at ten tomorrow, and it'll probably take me an hour to just get out of the driveway and the main roads. I'll see about getting your rental moved, though. My office is near where you parked it."

"Ah, your office. I heard you have another job, too. I mean, besides driving little old ladies around town, of course. You're not very forthcoming with information, Dr. Reese."

His brows furrowed. "It's not intentional. I'm not used to talking about myself and you were chatting with Gigi, I assumed she mentioned that I run the medical practice in town with her son, the other Dr. Bishop."

"A man with many hats," I said, stifling a yawn. "You must be pulled in every direction."

He shrugged. "It's not that bad."

Max lingered and I wasn't sure if he wanted to continue talking, or if he was just looking for an non-awkward way to escape.

"Well, for what it's worth, I came to Hope Lake expecting a lot and so far, this place has delivered. You've done a great job."

He smiled, and rubbed the back of his neck. "Don't let Marjorie fool you, my mother mostly runs this place."

"Your mother?"

He tipped his head to the side. "Yes, Marjorie. I sometimes people don't naturally know that and I suppose no one mentioned that either."

I laughed. "No, but I get the impression that people assume that everyone knows everything around here."

"You'd assume correctly," he said, smiling.

I stifled a yawn.

"I'll leave you to it," he said, backing toward the door.

"Thanks, Max. I hope to see you soon."

In lieu of a verbal response, he smiled, and gave a little bow.

Strong and silent types were not who I usually found myself drawn to. There was something interesting about Max that made me eager to research more than just Hope Lake.

4

Chapter Four

The next morning, I woke up later than I anticipated, even with the sun streaming through the thin curtains. While I was well rested, I wanted nothing more than to curl up with the warm blankets and sleep an extra hour.

My stomach was not on board with that.

Suitcases were left packed, stacked in the other room, which meant my charger never made it into the bedroom. I tapped the iPhone screen, as if that would magically wake it up.

Tossing it back onto the bed among the pillows, I padded into the other room to find something to wear downstairs for breakfast. My laptop greeted me like a shiny gray beacon.

"I'll get to you, promise," I said to the empty room.

I pulled on fitted jeans, a thick cable knit turtleneck sweater, and a pair of Sorel boots that I threw in my suitcase last minute.

Glancing in the full-length mirror on the back of the door,

I looked ready. For what, I didn't know but at least I was warm.

The hallway was empty, as were the stairs and the lower level near the fireplace. A young man was at the reception counter on the phone, but when he saw me, I got a wave. An actual wave, side-to-side motion, excited and happy. Not just an extended hand in the air in acknowledgement.

I followed the heavenly smells of baked goods and bacon. Most importantly, though, coffee. "Thank goodness," I said, making a beeline toward the coffee station. I poured a cup and added my sugar and cream.

If it weren't for the sounds of the snowblower outside, I would think that it was just me and the one employee in the entire building.

The sunroom at the back of the home that they used as a breakfast area was just as stunning as the rest of the building. The room contained tall, framed out windows that appeared they would open up in warmer weather to overlook the expansive area of gardens below. Not that I could see anything other than snow-covered bushes, but the idea of what they could look like had my imagination running wild.

"Good morning," a familiar voice said from behind me.

Marjorie walked in, albeit slowly, carrying a plate of scones and a small silver bowl of clotted cream.

"Good morning! You're here early," I said, walking over to take the plate from her. I placed it next to the coffee urn.

"I do live here," she said with a smile.

"I just figured since you were up so late, you wouldn't be working this early." I pulled out a chair for her.

"Now, don't fuss over me. I'm okay. Just golden," she said

with a laugh, but took the seat anyway. "Now get your breakfast while the scones are warm. The cream just melts right over them."

I grabbed one of the scones and cream, my mouth watering.

"What are you writing? Can I ask that, or is it a surprise?" she asked, fussing with the edge of the tablecloth.

"Not a secret. My boss, the editor of the magazine I write for, is familiar with Hope Lake. She spent a summer here when she was younger. The way she spoke of it, I always wanted to visit."

"It is a great place in the summer. Hopefully you'll have the opportunity to return."

I smiled. "I would like that. The article is on the town. A feature describing the town, the formative years through modern times. I've heard this place has really come into its own."

She nodded proudly. "We are transplants, but it's been a lot of fun to see the praise heaped upon the local government for all the hard work."

"Tell me about that."

She stayed quiet a moment. "When Max first bought the B&B, no one thought that it was a worthwhile investment, including him. Emma Peroni from the town office, she's—well, I don't actually know what she does, if I'm being honest. She's one of those people who has her hands in everything. I think she's a driving force behind all of the progress.

"My point is, she had a vision for the B&B and Max, well, he wanted *something*. She matched him up with this place about two years ago now. Needless to say, it was the best thing he's done since acing medical school."

I stood, eager for another delicious scone. "Coffee?"

"Now, now, this is my job," she said, smiling but not saying no.

"Let me, I'm up already."

Joining her, she said thank you. and wrapped her hands around the mug I set down in front of her. "Go on, I like hearing about, well, everything you want to tell me."

Marjorie smiled proudly. "You must find this boring."

"Not at all," I said, honestly. "I like getting a full picture of everything for a story. That includes the people, the town, the businesses. The whole nine yards."

Her face softened, eyes watering a bit as if she was excited to talk about her son. I couldn't blame her, you could see the pride she had for Max. "He poured so much time and energy into the process. A lot of the work he did himself or taught himself. Business is business he said, and it's run like a ship. When he brought me here to help out, I was skeptical until he brought Ross back too. He was one of the originals from back in the day when the old owners had it. Over the last year, he's hired some of the others, or I did, and it all sort of came together."

I smiled. "I can tell you're so proud of him," I began before taking a sip of coffee. "You didn't mention last night that Max was your son."

She smiled. "I thought you knew. Lord knows Mancini and Gigi don't let anyone forget it. Maxwell is a bit of a project for them. He's single, handsome, a doctor. They're practically swallowing their tongues trying to get him involved with someone."

Marjorie looked at me expectantly.

"Don't get any ideas," I teased, wagging my finger at her.

"You don't think my boy is handsome?" she said with a frown, but there wasn't anything genuine about it.

Of course I do, I thought. I've got eyes and he is very easy on them. Regardless of her baiting, I felt my cheeks warm under her scrutiny. "He seems like a catch, but he also seems firmly rooted here in Hope Lake."

"I hope." She looked down at her hands and twisted the thin, gold band on her ring finger. "When Maxwell's father passed away a six years ago, I didn't think he would settle in one place for longer than a few weeks."

"What do you mean?"

Marjorie sighed. "He's always had a wild streak. You'd never guess it by looking at, or talking to him now, all tailored and sharp, but he was a hellion back in the day. Loved to travel and explore. When he was in med school, a mentor gave him the idea for Doctors Without Borders, and he jumped on it the first chance he had."

"Really?" I said around a mouthful of scone.

She nodded. "Yes. When his father was sick, I didn't see him for almost a year. I think the travel helped him cope with the illness but then when he—" She paused and looked out at the falling snow covering more of the garden area out back. "I should probably let him talk to you. It's his story."

I admired her restraint and her deep love of her son. It was evident in how she spoke about him. "How about a change of subject?" I suggested, picking up my plate. "Oh, where does this go?"

Ross popped in as if he were waiting for the exact moment I was finished. "I'll take it."

"Thank you, I would have handled it though."

He smiled. "Nonsense. You're our guest."

I turned back to Marjorie. "What's your schedule like today?"

She shrugged. "Nothing until later although judging by the way it's coming down, I won't be going anywhere for the book club."

"Oh, there's a book club in town? I'd love to join one or is it just once a month?" I asked, pulling out my phone and choosing the calendar. "Maybe December's will be early enough for me to catch."

Marjorie laughed lightly. "Let's see, Henry, he owns the bookstore and runs something like six book clubs a month. But I'm only in three."

"Only?" I said, exasperated. "I barely keep up with one at home and they meet every other month."

"Well, there's not much going on in the winter months. He does as much as he can, but he teaches at the high school and at the college one town over. Plus, he's trying to plan a wedding, which can't be easy when him and his fiancée are both so busy."

"Charlotte is the florist. I remember Gigi mentioning her last night and I saw Henry when he came to drive Gigi, Sophia and Mancini home."

Marjorie looked appreciatively at a stunning arrangement

in the center of the dining table. "One of hers," I asked, admiring the overflowing vase myself.

She nodded. "She's very talented. My Maxwell liked her for a minute."

That got my attention. "Really?"

Marjorie sighed. "Yes, but her heart was always with Henry. From the way Gigi says it. Childhood sweethearts."

Admittedly, and not even knowing them from Adam, I swooned. "I love stories like that."

"You should read the romance that's coming up for discussion next week. If it's still snowing, we'll do a Zoom."

Impressed, I made another mental note. "That's pretty serious for a book club, isn't it? Ours just skips a month if we're being lazy."

"There's one thing that I've learned about Hope Lake."

"What's that?"

"They take everything seriously."

5

Chapter Five

I tucked the blanket under my legs. "Why did I think writing outside, in the snow, was the answer?"

After breakfast, Marjorie left to cover for the young man that was at the desk. I found out he was an accounting major at the local college and Max gave him the B&B books to practice.

I sought out a quiet, inspirational spot to try and get a little work done. The key to that was leaving my now-charged phone upstairs. Ignoring it wasn't difficult.

Curling up on the soft yellow outdoor sofa seemed like a great idea. A Christmas blanket on my lap and the brisk air to keep me laser focused, I settled in. The lightly falling snow added to the ambiance, except... the eighteen-degree wind had me high-tailing it back inside.

In the grand entrance adjacent to the check in counter, the entire area was open and it was peaceful. I beelined right for the massive fireplace that was roaring to life thanks to some poking from Ross. He took one look at me and insisted on bringing me tea.

I settled in on the love seat, pulling the tufted ottoman over to me so I could stretch out. The jeans had been tossed back in the suitcase, and I had switched to soft cotton joggers for warmth and comfort after breakfast.

Cracking my knuckles, I placed the laptop on Santa's face that smiled up at me from the blanket I had on my legs and stared at the blank document and blinking cursor.

"Riveting," Max said from over my shoulder.

"What?" I asked, feeling the eagerness to cover the screen but there wasn't a thing to keep secret.

He pointed at the blinking cursor and blank document. "I particularly like your use of metaphor and the pacing is spot on."

I looked up at him, thinking that was the most he had said to me that I didn't need to pull from him. "Hardy har har," I quipped, and closed the laptop with a click. "I'm struggling. I've been staring at that same page for a week. I thought you had patients?"

"I did. Some cancelled because of the storm. It's good too because it's getting pretty sketchy out there. I came to plow out the driveways."

"Why?" I asked as he came around to sit opposite me in the opposing Queen Anne chair. He filled all of the it with his large body. He crossed one long leg over the other and leaned his head against his fist. He looked relaxed, casual, and . . . what did Marjorie say, "Don't you think my boy is handsome?"

Yes, I dare say he is.

I shifted on the couch and kept my head down knowing that my cheeks were lighting up, I could easily blame the fire in the hearth.

"Everything okay?" he asked, either unaware of my blushing or helping me out so I wouldn't be embarrassed further.

"Yep, fine. Just warm by the fire," I lied, pulling the blanket off of me.

"Stanford, nice," he said, motioning to my very ratty, well-loved sweatshirt.

I smiled. "It was nice. I loved it there. Where did you go to school? Your mom said you guys weren't from Hope Lake originally."

"No, I was born and raised in West Chester, near Philly. College was Cheyney and medical school, well, let's just say we would have been rivals."

"Harvard?" I asked, immediately knowing his answer.

He nodded. "Harvard."

I shook my head. "I won't hold that against you. I hear it's a decent school."

He threw his head back. "A rival is a rival. I admit, though," he whispered, leaning in closer, "I contemplated Stanford for a minute, but I didn't want to leave the East Coast."

I leaned my head back against the couch and closed my eyes. "Oh, you would have loved the California weather."

He snorted. "I probably would have but five hours away was far enough for my parents."

When I looked at him, his eyes held so much sadness. "Your mom mentioned your father passed away. I'm sorry."

He swallowed hard, as if a lump were in his throat. "He

did. She hasn't been the same. It's why I brought her here. Her family is all spread out and her friends from back home come to visit in the summer. She shows the place off."

"How did you end up here?" I asked, and I hoped my line of questioning came off as intended. Eager to get to know Max Reese, not just as part of a potential story.

"Is this for your article, or personal knowledge?"
"Both, either? Neither? Your call. I told your mom the same thing. I know my editor called someone in the tourism office to let them know I was coming to do this piece. I don't want anyone to feel like they can't be honest with me or that everything that is said will end up in the article."

"I don't have anything to hide. I think you'll find that this place is a bit of an open book. No one can keep secrets here. It's nearly impossible."

I soured a bit. "That could be dangerous."
He looked thoughtful. "Not in a bad way. I'm sure if you wanted to, you could, but everyone is always willing to help so if it was something bad, the town would collectively try and find a way to make it right."

That eased the anxious feeling. "I find that interesting. The whole concept of small towns has always been a bit of a mystery to me."

"I think that's part of what drew me here. West Chester is big and this is really the opposite."

"Which reminds me, how did you end up here?"

He grinned. "I knew Dr. Bishop from my years with Doctors Without Borders. He had put a call out to colleagues for some help after his mom had a bad fall. You met Gigi. She's a force of nature but it was bad for a while. He was always such a stand-up guy that I knew I had to come. I didn't intend to stay but I fell in love with the place."

The *place* not the Charlotte. Interesting.

"The rest, as they say, is history. He was busy, and the practice could use another full-time doctor. Hell, we have a pediatrician on staff now too."

"The ladies said that people have interesting ways that they end up in Hope Lake. I'm starting to believe them."

We were quiet for a bit, just two people watching a crackling fire in a hearth. I'm not sure when I dozed off, or even for how long, but when I woke, Max was also asleep in the chair, a peaceful look on his face.

"I didn't want to disturb you both, but you'll miss afternoon tea," Marjorie said, resting her hand gently on my shoulder.

She turned to her son, and while she had been gentle with me, she giggled and held his nose with her fingers. After a second or two, he coughed, and his eyes opened. "I hate when you do that," he groaned and rubbed his eyes. He looked exhausted, even after a short snooze.

"You two sleepy heads won't be able to rest tonight if you waste the afternoon napping. The snow has stopped, and the sun is shining bright. Great time for a walk around the property to show it off," she finished by kicking his boot.

"I thought you said it was afternoon teatime?" I asked, still groggy and confused.

"It is," she said with a smile, just as Ross brought over two reusable mugs and my coat, hat, and gloves. "All ready for you guys to venture out. The air will do you good."

"I can take a hint," I said, laughing when she pointed toward the door.

"We're ordering pizza and wings tonight. Ross is taking the quad to pick it up. You've got a few hours so take your time. Explore, take notes, be inspired!"

"Subtlety has never been her strong suit," he said, opening the door for me.

The sun may be shining, but the blast of frigid air hit me like a freight train. "I can see that, but she is just lovely. I've enjoyed my conversations with her."

"She's happy to have someone other than Ross to talk to," he blurted, and I gave him the hardest side-eye. "I mean, you're perfectly lovely, but it could have been—I mean—you could have been—you know what, I'm going to stop talking."

I laughed. "Good idea. Considering we're surrounded by snow and I played softball."

He slid a leveling glance my way. "Oh, really."

I raised an eyebrow as we descended the steps into the front lawn.

At the base of the main steps there were two planters with tall topiaries that were filled with white lights.

"Hey the tree in town is getting lit up tonight, right?"

He shook his head. "No, it's postponed until tomorrow. Can't safely get everyone into

town with the snow still coming down."

"Smart. Tell me about it? What happens?"

He turned, looking up at the pure white sky. Snowflakes caught on his eyelashes, and beard before melting into them. He looked like an advertisement for an outdoor magazine. I nearly said it but bit my tongue.

"It's a surprise. I'll drive you tomorrow to see it," he promised.

We were enveloped in the shadow of the large building. It really was grand from every

angle, and it made me a little dizzy to stare up at the rooftop against the clear, blue sky.

"I'm not saying I'm challenging you to a snowball fight, but I'm not, *not* saying it, either," I warned, backing up slowly toward the two large stone planters that sat on the edge of the wide staircase.

"You wouldn't."

Max walked back toward his truck. It was cleaned off and there wasn't an inch of snow anywhere around it from where he plowed himself a path.

"That's a bad move, sir. Unless you're fast, you're not near enough snow for a good pack."

"Camille, you're from California. What do you know about packing snowballs?" he said, launching himself behind the safety of the truck.

"Shit," I cursed, and took off back up the stairs two at a time until I was firmly planted behind one of the four large pillars.

I began forming snowballs as fast as I could. He wasn't making a sound, and I was worried that he had escaped somewhere on the other side that I didn't know about. "You've got the advantage. I don't know this property like you do," I said, trying to draw out where he went to start his snow ammunition.

Silence.

He was better at this than I thought.

"It's almost not fair," he said from my right, just as a ball hit me in the back of the head. I hadn't pulled my long blonde hair up, instead keeping it down, which in hindsight was a mistake because it was caked with icy snow.

"You're a cheater!" I howled before sending two misshapen snowballs flying in the direction I thought he was in.

"Missed! I thought you played softball?"

The snow was falling from my hair and down my back through the coat. It was absurdly cold, and we were acting like children. But it was fun. I was having a blast even though I was pegged three more times with expertly thrown snowballs.

"Have I hit you at all?"

"Nope!" he said, and this time I knew he was back over by his car.

I tiptoed across the snow as softly as I could, armed with as many snowballs as I could carry. Desperately trying not to laugh, I jumped to the back of the truck to catch him by surprise.

"Huzzah!" I shouted, before dumping all of the snow on top of his head. "I win!"

Sure, he was covered in snow. Yes, I was too busy celebrating the spoils of snow war to notice him standing quickly and administering a quick, epic takedown by sweeping my leg out from under me and sending me into a mound of snow that he plowed.

"You stink," I said, holding my hands up for him to give me an assist.

"Rookie mistake. Never challenge someone who grew up

surrounded with snow to a snowball fight," he said, grabbing my hands.

Instead, I pulled him down, so he landed beside me in the pile.

"You cheat," he mumbled around a mouthful of snow.

6

Chapter Six

At dinner, I didn't see Max. There was an emergency in the next town, but he did leave word with Marjorie that he would be around for breakfast in the sunroom tomorrow morning. She delivered it as an invitation, with a smirk and a wink, but I insisted it was just breakfast.

"Nothing is ever *just* breakfast," she said.

"This was a single-family home at one point, right?" I asked, my notebook at the ready.

"Correct. Most of the homes out here on the lake started out as family estates back in the 1800s. Now, the two that are left standing are both B&Bs. This one and the old Lovegood mansion on the other side of the lake. It's set deeper into the woods and isn't as big as this, but it's beautifully maintained."

"Interesting. I love this sort of information. I feel like it gets lost a lot in the shuffle."

Marjorie laughed as she passed me the pizza box. "You should meet Emma and Cooper then. You'd get an earful for sure."

"Cooper the mayor?" I asked, taking the box and passing it to Ross.

"Yep, one in the same. Emma, his wife, is the self-appointed town archivist, so I'm told. She's spent much of the last two or three years collecting information to include in the historical register. When Max bought this and started cleaning out the attic, she practically lived here going through everything. Which was great because I got to watch their son, Sebastian. And her mother, Sophia, was here as well. I got to know that group a lot, which was nice since I was new to town myself," Marjorie explained and this time, I was prepared with the notebook to jot it all down.

"Oh, I met Sophia. Seems like a nice lady."

"She is, she usually comes around on Thursdays for tea with the ladies, but depending on the weather, we may just see each other at the tree lighting."

"I'll have to make sure I'm around tomorrow then too," I said with a wink.

"I'm excited for this. Small-town Christmas sounds like something you have to see to believe."

"Every year it gets bigger. It's really something to see," she explained, eyeing the notebook. "What are the notes for? The article?"

I slid the pad closer to her. "I'm here to write a book. Or, at least I hope to. That's for me, but the article is my last piece for the *American Adventure* magazine I was working at before I came here. Once I turn it in, my hope is to start a full-time novelist career, but, I need to get my head on straight."

"Well, I'm interested in everything. If you need someone to read the article, or the book, I'm your girl," she offered.

"I appreciate that. I'll need to chat more about the town."

"Oh," she exclaimed, her eyes growing wide. "You *really* want to talk to Emma then. Especially for the article. I'm surprised she hasn't sought you out yet."

I laughed. "I know my editor reached out but I'm thinking, perhaps, the weather is preventing it."

"Trust me, Emma will find a way to reach out. Even if she's driving a quad up here by herself."

My slice of pizza hovered between the plate and my mouth. "Is that good or bad?"

"Good. Emma's is wonderful. The best person for the job she's in, and she keeps Cooper focused on moving the town forward. She's just *a lot*. So, be prepared for the interrogation. The good news is, she'll bring a dessert and flowers to try and butter you up. They'll all be your best friends in no time."

I scrunched up my face. "I'm not going to be bribed into writing something favorable if that's what they're thinking."

Marjorie cleared her throat. "Nothing like that. They're just good at playing to the strengths of Hope Lake. They'll make sure – even underneath all of this snow and Christmas magic—that you'll see what a gem it is."

That mollified me a bit. "I could use them for the research I need. If I get a bouquet and a slice of pie out of it so be it."

*

Sometime around midnight, I awoke to a scratching at my window. Rolling over, I turned on the small bedside lamp, lighting up the bedroom in a warm yellow glow. The spindly branches from the oak tree were rubbing against the glass thanks to the strong winds.

My stomach rolled. I wasn't hungry but I wasn't settled either. Shuffling into the living area, I found slippers and a long Stanford sweatshirt and headed down to the kitchen to rummage around. I hoped that no one wouldn't mind.

The saving grace was that no one else was in the main part of the B&B to witness my pillaging of the pantry, or my outfit. Ross and Marjorie had apartments in a separate building, and though I still hadn't seen exactly where Max's living area was, I was curious about that set up as well.

Following the hallway nightlights down to the kitchen, I only stubbed my toe once and made two wrong turns. Getting a tour was moving higher up on the list. I really should have done that on day one.

The kitchen was dark, save for a snowman nightlight and the light of the moon, and a few under the cabinet lights shone balls of light onto the marble countertops. The pantry was thankfully clearly labeled, including a large basket with a chalkboard label reading *guests* and a smiley face on it.

Pulling it out, I placed it on the large island in the center of the room, and with my phone's flashlight, I found two delectable treats to munch on.

"You mind getting me a granola bar while you're in there?" Max said from the doorway.

I dropped the small pack of tea crackers, and my phone clattered to the ground, turning the light off.

"Jesus, you scared me!"

He held up his hands as he laughed. "I'm sorry, I thought you heard me. You were too focused on snack retrieval to hear my loud boots thundering down the hallway, I suppose."

I grinned. "I am peckish and there was no way I was falling asleep without something to nibble on."

"Understood," he said, flicking on two of the lights so that the room had at least some light. "Care for some company? I make a mean cup of cocoa."

I nodded. "Cocoa sounds like the perfect combination with these biscuits. Need help?"

He shook his head and began grabbing what he needed from various cabinets. "I'm a pro at this."

"Oh, it's homemade," I remarked, seeing him pulling out *actual* ingredients, not just a packet of Swiss Miss like I would have done.

He turned and gave me a look that suggested he was mock-offended that I questioned him. "I learned from my girlfriend at med school. She was French."

"She must have been some teacher."

His body shook with laughter. "*Oui, oui,*" he teased. His hair was wet, either from the snow or a shower.

I pulled my bare legs up onto the stool to watch him.

"Did you just get home?"

He nodded, scooping a chocolate powder into the pot on the stovetop. "There was an accident in Mount Hazel, all hands on deck, I'm afraid."

"Do you often have to go to neighboring towns?" I asked, mainly curious about the distance between towns.

He shook his head, lowered the heat to a simmer and turned, crossing his arms over his chest. The movement drew my eyes down, and I cleared my throat, looking away. The Rolling Stones shirt was a bit too well-fitted, but I think he did that intentionally as it enhanced everything on his upper torso. The sleeves were pulled tight around heavy biceps; the right showing off a tattoo but what it was I couldn't tell.

"I don't have to go that often. Frank, Dr. Bishop, usually goes because he's got a great relationship with the doctors in Mount Hazel and Barreton, but lately he's been encouraging me to go so I can get to know the next generation, as he calls us."

"So, you plan on making Hope Lake permanent?" I asked, wishing I had my notebook with me to jot down his answer.

He lowered his eyes, staring at his bare feet. "You spoke with Marjorie, I take it."

I inhaled. "We talked a bit. She said you liked the travel. As a person who travels, I get it. No judging. Just wondering if this is your home base for now, or forever."

He shrugged. "For now, it's forever."

"Poignant."

Turning, he went back to stirring the pot with slow, calculated swirls. "It's the truth, though. Can anyone say what's going to happen in five or ten years? Hell, even next month might present a different scenario. I can say that right now, I would like to stay here. I've grown roots for the first time in a long time. My mom is here, and she has this place, and friends to keep her company. She doesn't seem as lonely and lost. Sorry, I'm rambling."

He finished stirring and added something else from a mini glass jug that he pulled from the depths of the fridge.

"I like rambling," I said, walking up to stand beside him. "It gives people an insight that you don't get when the buttoned-up guard is up."

He looked perfectly at ease and comfortable. "Do you think I'm buttoned up? On guard?"

I grinned, "I think you are when you want to be. I'd be

willing to wager there's another side to Dr. Reese that us mere mortals don't oft see."

Moving toward him, I leaned against the counter, not touching him but not actively avoiding it either. I was a firm believer in if it happened, it happened.

Being so close, I could smell his shampoo even over the headiness of the cocoa. Between us, there was an awareness, and I wondered if he felt it too. There wasn't a surge or bolt of electricity that you read about happening, but I was more than conscious of him.

I was staring at the opposite side of the room where a large wooden framed portrait of the lake hung. It looked like a window to outside it was such a crisp and clear image. I felt his body turn, and I looked up at him. His beard was more grown than before. I guess he was embracing the lumberjack look.

Let's be honest, it was working for him.

"Max, I'm a journalist. I ask questions in the hopes of getting honest answers. I'll take real over fake BS any day of the week," I said, honestly letting his arm touch mine.

"I feel the same way," he whispered, dropping in a single shake of some sort of reddish-brown powder. "Secret ingredient."

"Can't wait," I said, moving imperceptively closer.

"Your mom seems to love it here," I remarked, seeing Post-It notes from Marjorie left on different surfaces.

"Excuse me," he said, reaching around me to take a spoon from the drawer beside me. When someone is that close to you, instinctively you have a tendency to back up, but I was against the counter, and had no instincts to step away.

I would be lying if I said I didn't find Max attractive, but to what end? As he said, his roots grew in here.

Dipping the spoon into the pot, he fanned it with his hand before holding it up before my mouth. "Try a little. See if you want more, or less, spice."

I plucked the spoon from his hand, not wanting to turn anything into a sexually charged event. We didn't seem to need more kindling in that fireplace.

"It's good," I said, setting the spoon on the trivet beside the stove. "The spice level is good. I'm a fan."

"It gives it a little kick while being a good partner with the chocolate," he said as he turned off the flame and reached into a top cabinet for two mugs and took two peppermint sticks from a small jar near the refrigerator.

He stepped over to the tall pantry cabinets. Opening the doors, he reached in and pulled out a bag. "Marshmallows?"
I gave him my best *duh* expression.

"I figured as much," he said, opening the bag and dropping two large ones in.

"Counter or breakfast table?" I asked, taking some napkins with me.

"Follow me," he said, leading me out of the kitchen and into the main area of the house. We walked past the reception desk and to the barely lit fireplace in the main room.

"If you don't mind, I'll throw another on this to keep you warm."

I looked down at my bare legs. Was I sending signals here? Max followed my gaze, and as if reading my mind, raised an eyebrow.

"Cami. I'm not looking for anything here except someone

to drink spicy, minty cocoa with and have a conversation. I have sweats that you can borrow if that makes you feel better," he said, turning to walk away from the door.

"No, it's fine. I just didn't expect to run into anyone. I should have –"

He laughed. "You should have prepared yourself for the possibility of running into the only other person in the house at midnight?"

I rolled my eyes. "Okay, okay I know I sound ridiculous, but I'm a fan of managing expectations from the get-go. This felt like a peculiar will-she-or-won't-she moment."

"I didn't think of anything other than cocoa," he said, and while I believed *him*, I wasn't sure if I believed myself.

Marjorie's words about breakfast rang in my head again. *It's never just breakfast.*

It's never *just* cocoa with Max.

7

Chapter Seven

I wrote all morning. Then I spent an hour trying to remember the last time that happened. The last time I felt so inspired that I was convinced I got carpal tunnel from the marathon typing.

There was a level of eagerness for tonight. To see the town fully celebrate the holidays,

Or maybe it was the midnight cocoa and conversation with Max that helped. Perhaps it was the eerily peaceful and still snow drifts outside my window. Whatever it was, I got back up to my room at two and wrote until the laptop died a couple hours later. Thankfully, I remembered to save it and plug the laptop in.

It wasn't an article on Hope Lake, either. Though I had some notes on that, I didn't start writing it.

It was *the book*. In my head I had been referring to it as this sentient being for years. The albatross. My ball and chain. Whatever I could do to convey that I was trapped by this story that was in my head, and not on paper. I kept thinking of the first line while I made coffee instead of having a decent lunch downstairs.

The town collects people. Not in a macabre way but in that people often search for a belonging. To be a puzzle piece, or to find the puzzle that they fit into.

I didn't intend to base the book on or in Hope Lake, but I was finding that the more I thought about the story arc, the characters, and the ever-changing plot that it fit being set in a place like this.

There were plenty of notes, words of wisdom and anecdotes from the various conversations that I had with people. Even though she was a transplant, as she called herself, Marjorie was full of information.

The more I spoke to Max, the more I thought about what the ladies said the other night about visitors who end up staying having interesting stories. It's been at the back of my head and I keep coming back to it.

One thing was clear, I hadn't yet scratched the surface, on the wonders of Hope Lake and I wasn't sure if I would have the time to get it all in before the story was due.

The locals who had found out about my stay, and the article, had their own fair share of stories they wanted to share, but thanks to the weather, it was proving impossible to visit or have them come to the B&B for a chat.

The options of course were to delay the article and focus on the book, or just run with it with the caveat that I would update and add in another edition.

Which meant, delaying leaving, both Hope Lake and *American Adventure*.

There was a lot for me to chew on but first. Max.

He had left a note under my door. Admittedly, seeing his doctor scrawl across the B&B stationary had made me smile.

It had said that he got called back to Mount Hazel to check up on a patient and that he wasn't going to be able to make breakfast, but that we would have some visitors for tea. It was disappointing, but writing all morning made the time pass quickly enough that by the time I was on ten-percent battery on the laptop, it was time to get ready to head downstairs.

I dressed casually since it was all I really had with me, but I felt better than just plugging down into the sunroom with sweats on. My fingers were sore from typing, and if I was going to be taking notes for the next however long, I wouldn't be able to move them tomorrow. Recording on my iPhone was the next best thing. Listening back to the words in their own voices had a way of transporting you back to the exact time and the feelings you had listening to them.

As soon as I got into the hallway, I heard them well before I saw any of them.

Which is saying something because I was on another floor, at the furthest end of the hallway, clear across the building from a bunch of elderly women. My steps quickened. I clutched the phone and notebook in my hand, and thanks to habit, a pen was wedged in my swinging ponytail. The railing looked as though someone had just polished it and that it would be slippery. The urge to slide down it as I had when I was a kid was strong but ending up on an exam table with Max checking out a broken bone wasn't high on the list.

By the time I reached the last stair, they had all turned and smiled in my direction. Mancini stood by the fire in a way that made her look like she was holding court. I supposed in a way she was. They all seemed to follow either her lead, or Gigi's, according to what I sussed out. Gigi was on the end of the couch near the end table with a deck of cards in her hand. That would be interesting.

A few others that I didn't recognize were scattered throughout the various chairs, and Marjorie was at the head of the room, beside Mancini, and laughing about something.

"There she is. We've heard a lot about your writing. If you include me, and I know you will, I'm sixty—"

"Eighty-eight—" Gigi chimed in, snickering when Mancini glared at her.

"As I was saying. I'm sixty-five, very slender, naturally black hair, no gray, and resemble Elizabeth Taylor in the eighties. Not the nineties because her hair was too big then."

I looked side to side at the group. Waiting for one of them to crack up laughing or to tell me she was joking. When no one did, I swallowed the laugh that was almost out and clapped my hands. "Great, I'll make that note. Tea, anyone?"

I turned and made a beeline for the sunroom praying that it was all set up and ready to go. Plus, I moved quickly so I could laugh the entire walk there.

"Hey, hey, where are you in a hurry to? The ladies came to see you," Max said, coming out of a door marked Office.

I kept laughing. "I saw them. They're *a lot.*"

He chuckled and when he saw them coming, he pulled me into the office. "I know. They're the best, though. I'm sure you'll see that. They're good people."

I stepped in further to check out his office. "Is this yours or Marjorie's?"

He looked around. "All me. It's too boring for my mother. She has a room off of reception that she uses for *business*," he explained using air quotes.

It wasn't boring in the least, at least not in my opinion. Dark wood molding rose up to the halfway point up the walls. Hunter green wallpaper went the rest of the way to the crown trim at the ceiling. A single photo sat on the desk, and I was desperately curious to peek, but I didn't want to pry.

"It's not typical, I'll give you that. I expected trophies, plaques, and certificates hanging up heralding your achievements."

He smiled. "They're all in the closet. My mother wouldn't let me box everything up. My medical school diploma is at the practice with some other documents. Everything else is right back there," he said pointing to a closet that blended in with the wall. Had he not pointed, I would have probably missed it.

"May I?" I asked with a raised eyebrow.

"Be my guest. Am I being researched?" he said, leaning against the wide oak desk and crossing his legs at the ankles. His arms were on either side of his hips, and again I was struck by how broadly built he was.

"Football?" I asked, stepping toward the closet. Opening it, I shook my head in disbelief. The closet had shelves along the wall filled with photos, diplomas, certificates and trophies.

"Wow! I can see why she wanted you to display them somewhere. There's a lot."

"To answer your question, no to football. Yes, I'm built for it, but I excelled in other areas of high school and college."

"Such as?" I asked, peering at some of the certificates. "Mock trial? Student leadership, band? You were in the band?"

He picked up the photo that I was curious about on his desk and held it out to me. I practically tripped to get out of the closet to grab it.

The photo was of perhaps a college-aged Max with Marjorie on one side and a Max look-a-like on the other. "You look exactly like your father," I said, admiring the man in the photo. He had the same deep brown eyes and strong jawline, but Max's was covered with a large white hat and a chin strap.

"Is that a tuba?"

He nodded and peered over at the picture. "Yep. Sixteen years of tuba lessons. It takes a big guy to carry it in parades and on the field. I had the build for it. My dad was in a jazz band back in the day. I guess I wanted to continue the love of music."

"I'm impressed. You must have been quite the student judging by the closet o' Max back there."

"I had my moments. The ones that, as my mother said, made her gray before her time, but I like to think I snapped out of it. I did make it through medical school after all."

"Max, according to that plaque in there, you did more than make it through."

He shrugged, suddenly bashful. "Like I said, I did okay."

A knock sounded before the door swung open and Mancini sailed through it, Marjorie hot on her heels looking eagerly between her son and I.

"Oh, you two look cozy. Are we interrupting anything?" Mancini asked before resting her hands on her hips.

I rolled my eyes. "Yes, you did. Max was about to throw me up on his desk and make wild, passionate love to me while you guys were down the hall sipping tea and having cucumber sandwiches."

Max choked. Someone in the hallway laughed, and Mancini clapped her hands.

But, Marjorie's reaction was what gave me the giggles. She looked wildly disappointed, with furrowed brows, and her lower lip jutted out.

"We're having sandwiches!" Gigi called as she zipped down the hall, ignoring the rest of my statement.

"I told you there was nothing going on," Marjorie insisted, still sounding disappointed. She pinched Mancini's arm. "Come on."

But when she turned to close the door, she gave Max a curious look.

And then winked.

"Let's go before they start rumors that will have the entire town talking," Max said, waving his arm for me to go first.

"Rumors don't get traction until someone denies them. That's when I find that everyone starts talking."

"Well, then, if someone asks, I'll just smile," he said, smiling, and the twinkle was back in his eyes.

8

Chapter Eight

Tea with the senior circuit of Hope Lake was a trip high-light, for sure. It was also something that could easily have been included in their YouTube shows. A weekly event I found out that they operated from their bakery, The Baked Nanas. The spot I stumbled into the first night I was in town. It wasn't just the group of ladies; we ended up being joined by Emma Peroni, Sophia's daughter and the brains behind a good portion of the *amazing things*—Sophia's words—that happened in town. Her husband and Hope Lake Mayor, Cooper Endicott, had dropped her off before taking their son, Sebastian, to visit his other grandmother, Clare. The Governor. There was a story there that I was interested in get-ting another day. Apparently, Clare and Cooper were Hope Lake royalty of sorts as her great-great-something-or-other founded the town back in the day.

From Emma I had heard about Charlotte Bishop, Gigi's granddaughter, and her best friend, Parker, who Emma called the money-lady, who I recognized from the Food Network.

Sitting at this table of pretty bad-ass women of all ages, I was taken aback thinking about the words I wrote earlier.

The town collects people.

The more I thought about it, the more things clicked into place. I was starting to think that the place was built with magic. As if it conjured up the people that it needed for that exact moment in time and then it hoodwinked them into staying by making them fall in love.

Huh.

Charlotte, who looked tremendously like a younger version of Gigi, was stuck at her shop and over FaceTime was talking Marjorie through rearranging the tablescapes as she called them, on each of the tables in the sunroom making sure they were angled *just so* to get the most out of the budding blooms. "I will change those out over the weekend, Marjorie. They're looking like a little sad sack."

"Whatever you think, Charlotte," Marjorie answered, before hanging up.

The others sat, sipped their tea, and chatted.

Emma was petite and stunning, with long chestnut hair and big brown eyes. She looked almost like a doll with model-like features..

"I've read your stuff before. I like the magazine," Emma said, sitting beside me and casually glancing at the scribbled text in my notebook. "Solid writing, eye for detail. What are you going to say about this place?"

Mancini chimed in before I could. "That it's gorgeous, turn of the century chic with all the modern amenities and a super attractive, and deliciously single owner who also happens to be the town doctor."

I held up my hand. "Hold on a second while I write all of that down exactly as you said it," I mimed writing it down in the air.

"You should leave out the part about Max being single. We don't want to get people's hopes up only to find out he's attached," Emma said before slyly high-fiving Mancini.

It took every ounce of control I posessed to school my features. It was bait, lobbed out by well-meaning, yet nosy, ladies trying to get a rise out of me. I wouldn't react.

I carried on as if they hadn't said a thing.

"As I understand it, you're the reason that Max has this place? How did you manage that? He must be busy enough being a young, hot doctor in town without needing anything else on his plate."

"Interesting choice of words there, Camille," Gigi said, tapping Emma on the shoulder.

Mancini inched forward. "What's the story?"

I thought back to what I said. "Super attractive, and deliciously single owner who also happens to be the town doctor. I don't get it, what's the problem? I'm using your words."

Mancini ginned. "Yes, but we said it without turning a shade of tomato."

I chuckled. "Oh, big deal. We all know the man is attractive, and I've heard the rumblings of what people say. He has a fan club—did you know that? Mancini,you even told me he's on the registry as *the* number one eligible bachelor in town."

"Well, that's not saying all that much. My son is on that list too," Gigi quipped, rolling her eyes.

"Seriously, though, Camille, have you given any thought to

taking a ride around the block with Max? He's very swoony," Mancini suggested.

I fought back the blush, to no avail judging by the looks they were giving me. "I'd be lying if I said I didn't think about, it but I'm here to focus on writing this feature, and hopefully a book if all goes well."

"I think it'll go well. All of it, too, not just the writing," Emma said, and I couldn't help but say a little wish that she was right.

*

When Max got back to the house after his last patient visit, he found me wandering around the library. It wasn't anything overly grand or massively fancy as most of the books had wandered off over the years, but they did have a decent collection thanks to visitors leaving things behind as regifts.

"Did you know Charlotte's grandfather was a writer?" he asked from the doorway.

I turned to see him leaning against the thick doorframe with a smile and a cup of something in his hand. "I made more cocoa. Travel cups so we can take it to see the lights."

"Oh, I was hoping that was what you had. I've been itching for it since the other night." I crossed the length of the room to greet him at the door. "Thanks, and, no, I didn't know that about her grandfather. I'm finding that this place is full of surprises and fun facts."

"I'm still learning them myself, so I'm sure you could teach me a thing or two," he said and took a seat in one of the reading chairs near the fireplace.

"Long day?" I asked when I saw him lean his head back

against the chair. Beneath his eyes were shadows, a few age lines, and more growth to his already thick beard.

He nodded, forcing a smile. Exahustion was all over his face.

"We don't have to do the tree lighting tonight. Or, I can hitch a ride with someone else. You're so tired," I offered, and he immediately sat up, as if the twenty seconds between sitting and my offer somehow rejuvenated him.

"I promised lights, caroling and I already made this cocoa. It would be terrible if it got wasted."

"Terrible," I said, smiling when he stood to extend his arm for me to loop mine thorugh.

"Besides, no patients tomorrow. Free day."

We exited the library and headed outside, down the stairs, our arms still linked together.

"Wow, what a novelty. What do you plan on doing with it?. Sleeping I hope," I said, taking a sip of the cocoa.

It was a little spicier than the first batch he made, but I liked it. "You should put this on the menu," I said as he held the door open for me. "I think people would love it."

"Maybe I will. I'll talk to Ross, and there's no such thing as sleeping in. I haven't been able to do that, in, well, forever. I was never much of a sleeper."

"Not me," I said with a laugh.

He closed the door and walked over to the driver's side. The Range Rover was already on, and warm.

"So, you're a sleeper?"

I thought about my answer as he pulled out of the drive and onto the main road that I felt like I hadn't seen in days.

"I could waste a day in bed with a book, or a television full of crappy shows. As long as the pillows are soft and the curtains are closed."

His head lolled toward me while he was at a stop sign. "That sounds like a perfect day."

"You should try it," I said, and I felt the heat rush up. "I don't mean with me. Jesus, I am a foot-in-the-mouth kind of girl around you. I mean, in general. Hell, with someone without someone. Whatever you want. I'm going to stop now."

"You make me laugh, Cami," he said, with a yawn.

"We don't have to stay long," I said feeling guilty that he was clearly so tired, and still taking me into town to see the lights.

"I wouldn't miss it, even if you weren't with me but this makes it that much more worth it."

This time, there was no hiding the rush of warmth in my face, or in my stomach. I reached over the console, and rested my gloved hand on top of his. I could see him smile even in the darkness.

By the time we reached the center of town, it was completely dark – at least in the sky. Every other inch of Hope Lake seemed to be bright with Christmas lights. Max pulled behind a two-story brick building and parked in a spot labeled, Dr. Max.

"Ah, reserved parking. Convenient for when you've got a town full of people, three feet of snow piled all over and nowhere to park."

"What can I say, perk of the job," he teased, and slid out of the car.

He tapped the hood lightly when he saw me reaching for the door handle to let myself out.

"Thank you," I said, as he helped me down.

Christmas music was playing but I couldn't tell from where. It was a popular tune and someone was singing a bit off-key but it was great nevertheless. Holiday spirit didn't care if you didn't sound exactly like Mariah Carey.

He pulled my arm through his again as we made our way up the driveway and directly into the square where people milled about.

"Wow," I breathed, unable to think of something more impressive to say. "It's just . . . I'm so glad you weren't too tired."

He was watching me take it all in. There was something intoxicating about knowing that you're being examined and I thought about Max being newish to town too. I wondered what he thought the first time he saw the winter specatular.

People dressed in varying states of holiday, milled about sipping drinks, chatting and some even had shopping bags. The stores around the square appeared open but glancing up at the tall clock near the fountain, I wagered they would be closing in fifteen when it hit nine o'clock.

"There's always a popcorn stand, somewhere to grab cocoa and then someone from Mount Hazel came this year with their homemade chocolates. They're spaced all around the square."

"Yes, yes and yes," I teased, leading him toward the group near a bunch of young people with various instruments.

"School band?" I asked, as we stood off to the side so we weren't in their way as they set up.

"Yes, they play carols and the kids from the elementary school sing a couple songs. Then Fr. John says a prayer by the manger scene and then boom, tree lighting. A couple oohs and aahs, and then people scatter. It's actually sort of funny to see how it empties right after."

"I don't blame a single person. It's cold."

"The older people head home, the kids go to friends and our age range head's to Casey's for pizza, HLBC brewing company for beer or Notte's Restaurant by the river for some wine."

"Sounds pretty perfect to me," I said open-endedly bumping into his shoulder with mine.

Max led me around, introducing me to a couple people if they came up to him but mostly, we walked silently taking in the general splendor of it.

Christmas was big in Palo Alto but this, with the added snow and frigid temperature made it feel like it was a different level of holiday cheer.

At the small gazebo near a cropping of snow-covered trees, Cooper, the mayor, knocked on the microphone a couple times before it screeched loudly earning a groan from the crowd. One of the band kids did a rim shot and everyone laughed, including Cooper.

"The Annual Tree Lighting is one of the most time-honored traditions in Hope Lake and this year is no exception. We challenged you to bring the spirit of the holidays, and you all rose to the occasions. I want to wish all of you a happy, and healthy Hanukkah, Kwanzaa and Christmas season and with that, I will turn it over to Dr. Imogen Bishop to flip the switch!"

The spotlight turned toward Gigi was in her motorized chair, though it had a couple emellishments on it including white lights, and a piece of garland wrapped around the back.

The crowd began counting backward from ten when Cooper raised his hand.

When the final number was called, Gigi flipped the switch and the tree lit up, sparkling from top to bottom, including a bright and enormous gold star at the top.

"I'm sure L.A. and San Francisco have great traditions and gigantic trees like New York does, but this one..." Max began, but I cut him off.

"Takes the cake for the best that I've seen."

I turned to Max, looking up at him as he smiled down at me. Maybe I was cocoa drunk, or perhaps the lights, the merriment and little voices singing had me caught up in the holiday spirit but I felt happy and delirious .

Patricia's words came rushing back, 'Let yourself be swept away.'

Following her sage advice, I reached up, took Max's face in my gloved hands and kissed him softly on the lips.

"Thank you for an amazing night. I'll never forget it."

*

We should have talked about the kiss on the way to HLBC, or even on the way back to the B&B but we didn't. It was just a kiss.

Even my inner voice thought I was lying to myself. *It's never just a kiss.*

When we got back to the B&B, it was closed up tight, only a few lights on to allow us to easily navigate throughout the main floor.

"Well," I said standing in a way that I hoped was inviting. Or, at least as inviting as I could be in a flannel shirt, thick wool coat and heavy winter boots. Not too mention the seriously sexy winter hat, scarf and gloves.

Apparently, the vibe I was aiming for fizzled like a dud firework. "Good night, Cami," he said, leaving me on the stairs to watch him walk away.

9

Chapter Nine

Inspiration struck again. This wasn't the same sort of energy that I had this morning, when I was eager for the day, but frustrated energy that led me to bang out four thousand words in about two and a half hours. I didn't even hate them – which I counted as a huge win.

When I still couldn't sleep, I took the laptop and opened up to the pages that I was writing for my editor, Patricia to take a look at. It wasn't my usual type of piece—factual, full of photos, general information, and suggestions on what to see and eat.

Instead, it was more of a story. A different story than the book that I was writing. I was worried because I had no idea if she was going to go for it or not.

I was still tooling away with the pages hours later when I stumbled into the library again to try and kill time until it was socially acceptable to be awake and hunt for breakfast.

There may have been a moment when I dozed off just before sunrise, against the back of the chair because when I jolted awake, Max was sitting across from me with two cups of piping hot coffee on the table between us.

"Can I take a look?"

I shrugged. "Sure," I said, handing him the laptop and diving for the coffee.

Once Max had it and I and saw him beginning to read it, I got up to pace with the warm mug in my hand. It didn't bother me that he might not like it, that was always a risk you took when you put yourself out there, it was that he figured prominently into it, as were his mom and his business.

The entire piece was built around the people, not the town. Because they made up the town. It was the anecdotes Gigi shared about her granddaughter's journey back into Hope Lake. The candid way that Mancini talked about Parker, who owned The Baked Nanas, and how she described her comings and goings and what made her finally stay even though she contemplated being a resident of both Pennsylvania and her native New York.

I talked about one of their cohorts and how she came here after meeting and marrying her husband after only three weeks of knowing him. She had previously never left Barreton, one of the other local small towns.

This didn't leave out the history of Hope Lake. The research had me deep diving into a rabbit hole with information that Emma provided about how the original founders, Campbell and Lovegood, had originally sought to build the town on a completely different section of land but that their horses stopped on the outskirts of the woods here and wouldn't leave.

"Does it seem like crazy old wives' tales?" I asked, anxiously gnawing on my thumbnail.

He held up a finger. "I started over again," he explained, and had changed positions, now sitting and placing the laptop on the table in front of him. He used his finger to follow along as if memorizing it.

The pacing continued until, finally, he spoke up. "This is just..."

Terrible? Horrible? I've given you a very bad day?

"Incredible."

I exhaled and collapsed onto the floor beside one of the tall bookcases. "You have no

idea how much I needed to hear that."

"Well, I had no idea that they weren't originally settling here. How did you find that out? You're here a week!"

"See what happens when you go to Standford and not Harvard" I teased, ducking from the pillow he playfully tossed my way. "They don't teach you how to take forever unless it's a wildly in-depth story that needs months of investigation, sources, you know the drill. You get in, you get the information you need, you get out. It helps to have someone like Emma and her skills and resources pointing you in the right direction."

"But the whole bit about Mancini's husband. I had no idea. You really think this place has *something?*"

I shrugged. "Listen, I'm not a believer in much of anything. I'm not religious and I'm not usually a universe-lines-things-up-in-a-special-way kind of thinker either, but when pieces fall into place a certain way, even the greatest of skeptics has to scratch their head and ponder life's great mysteries."

"Are you going to send this to your editor?"

I nodded. "Eventually. It's not due, or even something she was looking for. I just mentioned it off-handedly and she said go for it."

"Send it. Now. Don't wait until you can tinker and toy with it. Do it so you can't back out of it."

Max pushed the laptop toward me until it was precariously near the edge and I had to get up to grab it. "Don't think twice, just send it," he encouraged, smiling brightly when I nodded my head.

"I've sent her hundreds of articles over the years. Why is this one making me nervous?"

I admitted, my heart skipping a beat when I pushed send.

"Because it's different? You said this wasn't like the normal pieces you send, and you have that sense of what if that you don't usually have. It's totally normal."

"Thanks for the diagnosis, Dr. Reese," I teased and swallowed thickly when his eyes flashed.

I guess calling him doctor lit a bit of a fire in Max. Was he thinking of the kiss? Of what could have happened afterward if he hadn't left me on the stairs.

"I should be going," he said, standing quickly and heading to the door. "I'll see you, later. Cocoa, Nine o'clock, in the kitchen with the moonlight."

"Perfect," I agreed. "Though, this sounds like something out of Clue."

He laughed. "Dr. Reese in the kitchen with the cocoa."

"Dastardly," I teased, wondering if there would be a repeat. Another potential kiss in the moonlight.

"Maybe by then you'll have heard from your editor," he said, before disappearing into the hallway.

I stayed in the middle of the floor until my back and rear couldn't take it anymore. I read and re-read the pages from the book that I had been piecing together. If I was feeling energized from sending the article, maybe she would also read the opening chapters of the book too.

But, I fell into the rabbit hole of re-reading. Each time I added a little something extra. I poured everything I had into it until it was eight fifty-five at night and I was fast asleep next to the laptop.

10

Chapter Ten

The following night, after hours of toiling away at busy work, I had come up with a plan. I had just lit the final candle in the center of the place settings when Max appeared in the doorway.

"What's the celebratory dinner for?" Max asked, coming into the dining room looking too handsome for his own good.

I never thought scrubs would do it for me, but I was wrong. Perhaps, I needed to see Max in them and a ratty Aersosmith t-shirt to fully appreciate the aesthetic.

"Me," I said, carrying the printed email out from my editor.

"What's this?"

"It's from my editor. I thought, well it's been a bit since we talked and I had a lot to fill you in on."

"I'm sorry, I've been busy and I wasn't sure what I was thinking—"

"Same. I'm in the same boat but I haven't had another job

to keep my mind occupied. I fell asleep the other night and slept through our cocoa date. I'm sorry."

"Don't apologize. It's probably good that we didn't see each other that night."

"Why?"

"We'll get to that later. I want to hear about this," he said, flicking the paper. "Is it good news?"

"It's probably not going to run as a standard article," I explained, and watched his smile slip until I continued. "They're thinking of running it for the big Spring issue."

"Is that a much bigger one?" he asked, keeping my shaking hands tucked into my pockets.

I nodded. "It's twice the print size for one, but also the advertising budget is almost quadruple. I could be the cover article. Well, not me, but you know. *My* piece."

"Oh, Cami, that's amazing! You must be beside yourself."

I nodded. "I'm just—I'm proud of myself. I hope that doesn't sound obnoxious, but I am. I've worked so hard for this and for this to potentially be the payoff, I'm just . . . I want to celebrate."

"I'm so proud of you," he said, placing the email on the table. "I got the other work you sent. I was going to knock on your door last night to tell you I read it but I got back so late, I didn't want to wake you."

I had printed the first ten chapters of what I had for the novel and left it on the front desk with his name on them. They were gone when I popped back down the following day, but still no word. I left my cell, email, and a brief apology for missing the cocoa date that I slept through.

"It was a good surprise," he said, walking over to the sideboard near the wall to take the stack of papers from it.

I didn't notice them when I walked in.

He handed it to me, and pulled out the chair. Sitting, I placed the pages beside me and noticed that he had made notes. "Oh, you marked it up."

Admittedly, it made me anxious until I saw that the marks were smiley faces or hearts near passages that he liked. Some spots were underlined or added exclamation points for emphasis.

"I take it you liked it?"

He took his seat, and with the candlelight, he looked eager, happy.

"Loved it. You mentioned something interesting in the article."

"Oh, yes? What is that?"

"Something very important that I would like to talk to you about. Something that your editor discussed with you."

"Ah, yes. That detail."

He was referring to a section toward the end of the article where I contemplated my role in the storied history of Hope Lake. Would I just be a visitor, or would I, too, be sewn into the fabric of the town like the others who came, fell in love, and stayed.

"She offered to put me in touch with an agent friend that she has in New York. If she like the book, maybe this is the start of a new writing career. It'll be new, but someone wise said just because you're scared of something new doesn't mean you don't do it."

"I think I would like that too. You know you'd have a place to stay when you're here, you know, visiting."

I grinned. "And if someone that loved to travel had some time off, they could come on some new adventures."

"This is a story that I really want to read the ending of."

11

Chapter Eleven

When you begin writing an article on a relatively unknown place, there's an extra bit of nerves to it. Especially when you've found yourself really loving the town you're in. Objectivity seems to be out the window.

Logic and brutal honesty are things of the past but that's okay. Maybe, just maybe, that's what the world needs a bit more of these days.

Fun, simplicity, kindness.

All of those things you'll find in Hope Lake. A small, secluded section of Pennsylvania you'd drive right past if you weren't looking for it.

But, oh, how you should be looking for it.

You don't have to be a great outdoors enthusiast, or a fan of antiquing. Maybe you're just looking for a spot to escape that makes you feel at home the second you cross into town.

The people are some of the kindest I have ever met. Hope Lake isn't lacking for the rich, or the famous. It's steeped in creative and hardworking people, and they want everyone to know just how much this town means to them.

How much it now means to me.

I fell in love enough to move across the country and start a new chapter of my life, both career and personal, and for all intents and purposes, I have Hope Lake to thank for it.

So, I'm signing off of *American Adventure*.

From Hope Lake, With Love,

Camille

12

Epilogue

Five Years Later

Emma

"Cooper, it's time to make the toast!" I told my husband as he held onto our squirming toddler, Carter. Our older son, Sebastian, was tickling his brother's pudgy little feet as his father struggled to balance a toasting glass, and the chubby baby.

"Yes, Madam Mayor," Cooper said, smiling at me.

Madam Mayor. It had been a little over a month since the election, but I still wasn't used to the title. I wasn't sure that I would ever be. Who would have thought after all my reservations about running for office myself, that I would do it, and win.

Politics, one could say, were so deeply ingrained in both Cooper and I that our friends said it was inevitable that I tried my hand on a campaign for myself.

Thankfully, I didn't have to run against my husband, I'm not sure how that would have worked out for our marriage.

Cooper had his sights set on higher office and when his second term as Mayor was over, he decided to take time off to spend with our children, but also began to put a team together to help him run for Congressman.

When he won, cause let's be honest, my husband would not lose, it would be a lot of strain on our growing family—the traveling to DC and the hours—but true to the fashion of the Hope Lake community, everyone rallied when we announced our plans.

My parents, who spent the last few years traveling, planned on helping us raise the kids while we pursued higher levels of public service. It's not as though we weren't already busy, but this would present a whole new world for us.

Cooper cleared his throat, and Anna, our three-year old daughter who was sitting beside him in her booster seat, laughed loudly. "Thank you, Anna for that lovely introduction."

"Family. Not friends, family and loved-ones, what would we do without you? We are blessed that you're all with us here to celebrate the holiday season."

Our family, immediate and very-extended, sat together at the beautifully decorated table in our family home. Over the years, the table had grown from one, to two, to three spanning across the dining room and sitting room beside it. We wouldn't have it any other way.

To my right sat, Charlotte, Henry and Imogen Mercer, their daughter who was only two weeks older than our Anna. Across from them was Charlotte's father, Andrew and an empty seat beside him in honor of Gigi.

"Even those that we've lost are here with us today," he said, his eyes sliding to the empty chair. "In the laughter of our children, and the joy in singing carols," Cooper began, before pausing to swallow the lump of sorrow I knew had lodged in his throat over Gigi's loss. Charlotte's eyes teared as Henry took her hand comfortingly. We were all still mourning the loss of our beloved Gigi who had passed away just a day after celebrating her one-hundredth birthday in October.

Just as she wanted, she made it to a hundred and passed peacefully in her sleep. The loss rippled through town and was felt so profoundly due to Gigi's long-storied career and because she was well-loved by so many people.

"Since it's inception, Hope Lake has been about new beginnings, family, progress and welcoming to every person who finds themselves lost and looking for a new start.

Hope Lake wasn't short on newcomers. Though, at this point, the newer residents at the table had been here for years at this point.

Camille and Max Reese sat beside Marjorie, Max's mother who helped him run the B&B.

Parker Powell and Nick Arthur were gazing at each other over the yule log that Parker baked for the holidays. True to Parker fashion, it wasn't just the log, but also four different pies, a trifle, and three types of truffles.

One thing that was common among all of them was that they were in search of something, and found it here, in Hope Lake.

"My hope for all of you, is that whatever wish that you hold deep in your heart comes true this holiday season. Hope Lake isn't short on magic, especially this time of year."

"Merry Christmas, Happy Holidays and stay hopeful."

Acknowledgements

A humble thank you to everyone who has fallen in love with Hope Lake. It's been a joy to explore what, in my mind, is a fun little small town in America. It is based, in part, on the area I grew up in, and continue to live in today. The best of all the small towns around me.

Many thanks to my wonderfully patient and kick-ass agent, Kimberly Brower. My friends who have helped so much along this journey through the author world, especially Sylvain Reynard and Debra Anastasia.

To my local friends, and family, who were kind enough to share funny stories and read early drafts and for the encouragement to chase dreams.

And finally to the real life Golden Girls in my family; Lillian, Pauline, Dinah, Clara, Mama Gloria, and Suzie. I am endless grateful for the love, support and badassery that you have passed along.

XO

Neens